THE MELODIES OF LOVE
BY: Balinda I. Multimore

ISBN -13:9781544196640

Gratitude from the Author

I thank God the creator, for giving me a brilliant mind, the wisdom to use it, family and friends.

I thank my mom, Girtrue Haywood, for always believing and supporting me. In 1993, I performed my first public poetry reading, my mom brought my three kids to see me. Throughout my poetry reading career, she attended every event I participated in. Mom your presence and your love helped to ease my fear.

I thank my husband Steve Multimore for buying me my first computer from Radio Shack. In your own special way, you believed in me. Thanks for giving me some feedback on this book.

I thank my three children, Shywyona, Steve, Jr. and Lewis Multimore, thanks for always rooting for me to succeed as a writer. You are my inspirations, that keeps me going when I want to quit. Now I have 3 additional inspirations, my grandsons, Jermaine, Jr., Jeremiah, and Columbus.

I thank my family and friends, for your love and support.

I thank Norman Drittel, owner of Love Greeting Cards, in 1993, he hired me to write 4 prose, that was less than 25 words in total. I made my first $100.00. He told me I had the niche for writing.

The Path That Led the Author to Writing This Book

In our lives, God allows special people to cross our paths to help bring out the gifts that were instilled in us. My life was filled with some of these special individuals who believed in me as a writer. However, none of them pushed or challenged me as hard as my good friend Althea Lamar. In 1983, she planted the seed in my mind that I could write my first novel. Her insightfulness into my abilities to write The Melodies Of Love, was based on several conversations we shared and my poetry. I didn't take heed at first if the truth is told, I didn't believe I could do it. I wrote the first draft of this book before Althea passed away. It took twenty-seven years for me to give birth to The Melodies of Love. My belief and my desire finally got in alignment with each other.

I would like to thank the four women who allowed me to interview them with one question, that helped to give me some insight into writing this book.

Thoughts from the author to the reader

Though the characters in this book are fictional, the experiences they go through happens in real life. As babies, we yearn to be loved and to feel the comfort of being in the arms of our parents. Our parents love is like a security blanket; they are our first introduction to love. As we get older we still yearn for love and that warm touch, except we seek it from strangers. When we first get involved in a romantic relationship, the person starts out as a stranger. Over time we learn about the person's character and it's those characteristics that we fall in love with. Once we've fallen in love, love sometimes leads us down the aisle to marriage without knowing what the other person's interpretation of love is. Just remember love adds to your life, it doesn't subtract from it!

There are different types of expressions of love; love of family, friends, man, woman, partners, love of oneself and last but not least the love of God.

Quotes of expressions of love to me from my husband, children, my mom, family, and friends.

"I know when I first saw you, walking across that football field in high school, there was something special about you." My husband Steve (he was right- 34 years later)

"Love bends it never breaks" and "Mom loving you is easy." my son, Steve Multimore Jr.

"Mom you are my queen, my teacher about love and life and my best friend." my son, Lewis Multimore

"I love You", "Me and My three sons thank you for all you do." my daughter, Shywyona Carson

"I thank God for giving you a lot of patience and love for others." My mom Girtrue

My nieces and nephews, who always said "I love you", every time we meet.

My mother and father- in law Mattie and James who said, "We love you," after every telephone conversation.

"Thank you for being a good friend to my mom and she to you. I hope one day I will have the kind of friendship you shared." Kayla; "Every time I talk with you, I'm inspired." Ms. Bonita

"Mrs. B., I miss your laugh, your ways, talking to you about my problems, you are a special person. This is from my heart and you know I'm not a mushy person, but you hold a special place in my heart. Thank you for being you." Raquel

"Thank you for being a part of our lives." Joyce, Maritza, Ana, and Tyneisha

"You are so amazing. I love you so much my sister. I am so honored to have you as a mid-wife in my life to help push me into my destiny." Natascha

"I'm grateful to everyone who helped me to evolve into the person I am." The Author, Balinda

Chapter 1

Usually, Friday afternoon traffic jams didn't bother Jackie. However, today she wasn't in the mood to deal with any "road rage" drivers honking their damn horns or cutting her off in traffic. The only thing on her mind right now was how belligerent Michael became over the phone earlier that day. She merely mentioned going to Happy Hour at the Oasis Lounge tonight with Janice and Roxanne. His voice escalated and he began speaking to her like she was a woman in the streets instead of the woman he was in love with. "What do you need to go out clubbing for, when you already got a man? All the money I've invested in you, I'll tell you what you better do, you better stay your ass home and spend time with me!" said Michael.

Jackie was speechless and hurt. Jackie didn't respond to any of his nasty insults. She hung up the phone in his ear, ran to the storage room and begin crying. How could this man who says he loves her say such hurtful things? Jackie thought. She had spent the past two years catering to his selfish needs. She had spent almost every weekend doing something with Michael. She never once complained when he wanted to hang out with the fellows and even then he wanted her to be in place when he called.

Exit 96 was finally in-sight and Jackie's mind was calculating the confrontation that might be waiting for her with Michael. These thoughts cluttered her mind until she nearly rear-ended a blue station wagon that had come to a sudden stop, allowing a dog to cross the street. Jackie started cussing out loud to herself. If that excitement wasn't enough, she pulled her red BMW into the parking garage of her apartment complex and there was Michael's Misty Gray Cadillac parked in the visitor's parking lot.

Her heart hammered against her breast; she didn't know what to expect. She sat in her car and took a long pause before getting out. She slowly walked over to the elevator. The anxiety from fear overwhelmed her body. Michael had never spoken to her in that tone of voice. This was a familiar feeling of fear she had experienced when she was younger. She witnessed her father verbally abusing her mother. His voice was so loud that it seemed like the entire neighborhood could have heard him yelling at her mom. She finally reached the 4th floor, where her apartment was.

She strolled down the hallway, dreading the moment when she reached her door. She put her key into the keyhole, turned the doorknob slowly, then peered around the door. Michael was nowhere in sight.

"Thank God," Jackie thought. She tiptoed into the bedroom. There his black ass was, stretched across the bed and butt naked. "Come over her baby and let me give you something that's better than Happy Hour," he said. If looks could kill, Michael would have been dead from the pissed off look Jackie had on her face. Jackie stormed out of the bedroom, slamming the door behind her. She was mad as hell!

Michael came into the living room. "What's your damn problem?" he asked as if he had no clue. "It's best you leave," said Jackie. "You're an ungrateful bitch; after all, I've done for you," Michael yelled. Michael picked up Jackie's favorite crystal vase and threw it against the wall. The vase hit the wall with the force of a fastball and shattered into a million tiny pieces. Jackie looked down at the fragments scattered across her brown tile floor. Then she looked up at him, standing in the doorway with nothing but his boxer shorts covering his partially built body.

Tears rolled down her pecan colored cheeks. Her blood pressure began to skyrocket. Those five-hundred-dollar silk Italian suits or those $300 Michael Jordan sneakers couldn't conceal this simple-minded man. If he thought, she was going to put up with this type of bullshit, he was most definitely wrong. Her father controlled her mama through fear, however, she'll be damned if it was going to happen to her by a rich or poor man. If she gave into fear now, fear would control their relationship, she put that shit on the back burner.

Yeah, Michael had a damn good job. He has been working as a computer programmer at Zenex-Microsoft for the past seven years and as a firefighter part-time. Sure he spent a hell of a lot of his money on her. They dined at some of the finest restaurants Pie County had to offer. The Starlight Restaurant by the ocean was one of her favorites, it was top the of line and you couldn't order anything under $50. They ate there at least twice a month. She especially enjoyed those weekend get-a-ways to the Bahamas and Las Vegas. She also enjoyed receiving those forget-me-not presents like the ½ karat tennis bracelet and matching diamond stud earrings he had given her. But he enjoyed those I-can't-wait-to-see-you-in-it negligees. Honestly, what woman enjoys a string caught between her crack while trying to make love. She sure as hell didn't!

He gave her money to pay her rent. Hell, as much as the man was sleeping over there, you would have thought he lived there as well. But she'll be damned if he thinks all of that has brought him ownership of her. Money buys material things, not people.

Michael quickly put on his pants, all the while cursing up a storm. "You think I need to put up with your shit? I don't need a woman who doesn't listen to me. There are a lot of women just waiting to take your place."

"Just give me my keys," Jackie demanded. Those words must have set off a time bomb inside of him. No woman has ever rejected him. Michael felt like he had been used and now she was throwing him out like yesterday's newspaper.

"I'll give you something all right," said Michael. The sound of those words filled Jackie's body with fear once again. Michael rushed toward Jackie and grabbed her by the throat pushing her back into her bedroom. She was kicking and hitting him. Jackie was trying to fight back, but to no avail, as her actions only enraged him more. He threw her down on the bed and pinned her arms above her head with one hand and began ripping off the Ralph Lauren Dress that he'd brought as a Christmas gift.

Jackie began pleading with Michael. "Please Michael just leave, don't hurt me, please don't," she begged. The look on Michael's face was cold that of a man with no emotions. "Hoe I'm going to fuck my money's worth out of you. You ain't getting rid of me that easy." As Michael was taking off his pants, Jackie tried to make a quick dash for the door, only to get caught by the leg and pulled her back onto the bed. He then picked her up and threw her on the bed and pinned her down. "Where the hell did you think you were going. I ought to kill you bitch, but you ain't worth going to prison for. The only thing you are worth is a good fucking. To think, I spent all my hard earned money on a bitch like you. I must have been a damn fool to have fallen in love with you."

Michael proceeded to pin her arms above her head, minimizing her struggling. Jackie continued to squirm and wiggle as Michael placed all of his weight on her lower body, in an attempt to cease her movements altogether. As strong as he was, he was able to keep her arms pinned with only one hand. She felt his other hand graze her crotch before he ripped off her pantyhose. Jackie's heart began to beat a mile a minute as she felt his bare body against hers, without warning he rammed himself into her. He held her arms, viciously stroking into her, as a rapist would. Sweat dripped off of him and onto her like a dripping faucet. The harder he stroked, the stiffer Jackie made her body, making Michael's insides burn with fury. "You're lying there like a dead woman. I got something that will bring your ass back to life." As Michael was flipping Jackie onto her stomach, she started squirming her body back and forth, hitting him in the face a few times. Michael punched her in the eye. "Lie still before I really hurt you." He grabbed her hands and flipped her over onto her stomach. He wanted to cause her pain. She felt his penis rub against her ass cheeks as his knees opened her inner thoughts. He was going to shove himself into her rectum. Just as he began to penetrate her rectum, something inside of him wouldn't let him go through with it.

He got out the bed, put his clothes on and told Jackie she caused this ordeal on herself. He threw her keys on the bed and strolled out the bedroom never looking back at Jackie once. When she heard the sound of the front door slamming she knew he was gone.

Jackie slowly got up, sat on the of the bed crying and in pain. She felt like a rape victim. She went into the bathroom and took a hot shower to calm down. The phone rang and she nearly jumped out her skin. She got out the shower and answered the phone.

"Hi girl, are you ready to party tonight? Janice and I will be there to pick you up in 20 minutes." Roxanne asked. "We can do the

Oasis thing another time, I'm going to stay in and rest," Jackie said. The trembling sound of Jackie's voice made Roxanne think something was wrong. "Are you all right Jackie?" Roxanne asked. "Yes, I'm ok, just a little tired," Jackie replied. "Girl you sound awful and we are coming over there to check on you," said Roxanne. That was the last thing Jackie didn't need to happen, was for the girls to see her black eye. However, Roxanne insisted on coming over, she refused to take no for an answer.

Jackie quickly rushed into the bedroom and slipped on her sleepwear. She took a long look at her black eye in the mirror. There was no way to hide it. She wanted to call the police but thought it would sound stupid. "Hello, I would like to report a rape. By whom ma'am? My boyfriend." Those people would probably want to know how did she get involved with a lunatic like that.

Roxanne went to Janice's house and picked her up. Once in the car, Roxanne explained to Janice why they were not going out tonight. Janice had no problem with checking on Jackie to make sure she was okay. There was a hard knock on the door that startled Jackie. She looked in the peephole and saw it was Roxanne and Janice. She opened the door to let them in. They took one look at Jackie's eye and knew someone had punched the shit out of her.

Janice quickly asked, "Did Michael do this to you? Cause if he did, you better put that bastard in jail." Roxanne threw her arms around Jackie to comfort her. Jackie told them every detail of her ordeal in between crying. Janice hollered, "Did you call the police yet?" "No, I was a shame to call," Jackie replied. "Give me that damn phone, I'll call 911!" Janice said. "No man has the right to put his got damn hands on a woman and if you don't stop him now some other woman will have to live through this type of hell," said Janice.

Jackie's pride took a back seat, she no longer thought it was embarrassing to call the police. Domestic violence cases were taken seriously when there was visible evidence that a crime had been committed. The perpetrator would be arrested. Jackie's black eye was the evidence that a crime had occurred.

When the police came out to take her statement, it was very hard for Jackie to speak about the incident. Almost every other word was followed by tears. These two male police officers were sensitive to crimes of this nature. Jackie gave them a detailed statement of the incident starting from the time she entered her apartment. One of the officers told Jackie to go to Carl Hopkins Hospital to be examined for the rape allegations she had made. They had an excellent rape treatment center there. Jackie agreed. Jackie slowly got dressed with the assistance of Roxanne and Janice. They went with her to the hospital. Janice and Roxanne waited for Janice in the waiting room. Being in the hospital brought back some raw emotions for Roxanne, from her near- death experience.

Doctor Tracey Moore was the director of the Rape Unit at Carl Hopkins Hospital. She likes to talk with each rape victim personally. While Jackie was waiting in the room to be examined, Doctor Tracey walked in and asked her how was she doing. Jackie responded, "fine". "I'm Doctor Tracey Moore and I want you to know you are in good hands, at Carl Hopkins Hospital. A smile came upon Jackie's face as she shook the doctor's hand.

Doctor Moore explained the procedures that were going to take place and asked Jackie if she had any questions. Jackie told her no and told her about the altercation and rape. Doctor Moore gave her a hug and told her things would get better. She asked her if she believed in God and Jackie said told her yes. Doctor Moore said a prayer with Jackie and told Jackie that the God inside of her was bigger than any situation on the outside. Jackie nodded her head in agreement.

Doctor Moore gave her a referral to speak with a rape counselor. As the doctor was getting ready to leave, she told Jackie they would do an AIDS test, it was a routine procedure. Jackie looked a little startled, at first but agreed. Another doctor came in and examined Jackie with the rape kit and drew blood. Jackie got dressed and waited in the waiting area with Janice and Roxanne for the results.

While in the waiting room Jackie received a phone call from Shira, the paralegal who worked at the Pie County State Attorney's Office, DCU satellite office located inside the police station. She, informed her that Michael was in custody. The nurse called Jackie into the back room with the results of the AIDS test. It came back negative. Jackie was relieved, however, after the examination, and going over the details of the ordeal again with Doctor Moore she felt worthless. Jackie couldn't wait to leave the hospital.

On the drive to Jackie's house, Roxanne and Janice asked her if she wanted them to stay the night. Jackie told them no. She would be fine. Tomorrow she was going to her sister's house and spend a few days over there.   They dropped Jackie home. Once inside Jackie poured her a class of Bertani Amarone Wine and sat on the couch. In her mind, she was wishing this incident with Michael was a bad dream. How could this man she was in love with commit such a horrible act against her. She sipped wine until she fell asleep.

The police officers arrived at Michael's condo and knocked on the door. Michael's ego was bigger than his balls, he had picked up his ex-girlfriend, Charlotte after he left Jackie's house. Michael was in the room changing clothes. He yelled out to Charlotte to answer the door. "Who is it"? she asked. The police ma'am. Charlotte went to the bedroom and told him the police was at the door.

Michael chuckles, what would the police be doing at his house. Michael went to the door. He looked out the peephole. "Who are you looking for?" Michael asked. "Is there a Michael Johnson here?" Michael opened the door and said, "Yeah that's me." "We have a warrant for your arrest." "There must be some mistake, Sir, I haven't committed any crime. I had a little misunderstanding with my girlfriend earlier." Michael said. One of the officers responded, Mr. Johnson, we don't call rape and a black eye a misunderstanding. We call it a crime here in Pie County.

Michael's robe came loose and he was still wearing those damn boxer shorts with red hearts on them. One of the officers remembered Jackie's detailed description of them. They had red hearts all over them. Mr. Johnson, we need these boxer shorts for evidence. Please remove them. Michael went into the bedroom and one of the officers followed him in there. Michael took off the boxer shorts and handed them to the officer. Then he put on another pair of boxer shorts along with his jeans and a blue T-shirt. One of the officers retrieved an evidence bag from the police car and put the boxers in the bag. They handcuffed Michael and read him his rights. "Charlotte, get out my house and lock it up," Michael said.   When the door closed behind Michael and the police officers.

Charlotte laughed out loud to herself. She had revenge written all across her face. Michael was a poor excuse for a man let alone a husband. He had dropped her like a hot potato a month before they were to get married, two and half years ago.

Her parents had spent two thousand dollars or more on her wedding preparations, and the money was non-refundable. Charlotte nearly had a nervous breakdown behind that shit. She had to seek professional counseling for six months before she could talk to another man. She was shocked, tonight when Michael knocked on her door. After two and half years, did he feel that she deserved an explanation for his sudden department out of her life?   The truth be told she was still in love with him. She was ready to listen to whatever far fetch lies he was going to tell her. Unfortunately, he was hauled off to jail before he had a chance to let the lies roll off his tongue. What Charlotte didn't know was that Michael was finally going to confess as to why he didn't marry her. He had gotten cold feet and he wasn't ready for marriage. Charlotte was a nice young lady but she didn't have the qualities he was looking for as a wife. Charlotte had no ambitions to do nothing more than work an 8-5 job and get a paycheck. Michael wanted someone who wanted more out of life, than a paycheck. However, like a coward, instead of telling her the truth, he allowed her to make a fool out of self.

While sitting on Michael's leather brown couch this wild idea came into Charlotte's mind. She called the computer company where he was employed, they stay open 24 hours a day. She pretended to be a police officer. "Hello, I'm Officer Pearsall and I'm calling from the Pie County Police Department. Can I speak to Michael Johnson's supervisor?" The receptionist connected her with Mr. Hank, Michael's field supervisor. Charlotte went on. "I'm calling to inform you, that one of your employees, a Mr. Michael Johnson was arrested". "What was he arrested for?" Hank asked. "He was arrested for domestic violence", said Charlotte. Hank was a little suspicious of the caller. When Charlotte hung up with Hank, he called the Pie County Police Department to find out if Michael had been arrested. The person at the police department told him, he had to contact the jail and gave him the jail telephone number.

Hank called the jail and gave them Michael's date of birth. The correctional officer researched Michael's information in their computer system and told Hank, Michael was in jail. Hank wanted to know what the charges were and he was told that type information couldn't be given out. Hang hung up the phone, with such disbelief of what he had just heard. Michael was being considered for a promotion as a supervisor. Now all that could be down the drain. Being arrested for any reason is grounds to be terminated, Hank thought to himself.

The next day Michael was able to use the jail telephone. He made a collect call to his good friend Carlton. Carlton accepted the call. Michael told Carlton that he would explain what happened later. He needed two favors from him. First, he needed him to bond him out of jail and secondly to make a three-way-call to his boss Hank. Carlton agreed. Michael knew Carlton had Globatel on his phone for his cousin to call him collect from jail.

Michael told Hank that he had a family emergency and wouldn't be at work for a few days. Hank didn't ask any questions he told Michael he needed to speak with him when he returned to work. Michael agreed. Michael was able to bond out of jail in 48 hours. Carlton posted the bond and bail bond's man bonded Michael out of jail. Once out of jail, Michael had to figure out how he was going to get home. He saw a stranger sitting on the bus bench and asked if he could use their telephone. The stranger handed Michael the phone and he called Lyft to get a ride home.

Once he arrived home he saw a big note on the bed from Charlotte. "I hope you get everything you deserve and don't you ever look me up again. Michael threw the note in the trash. Then he took a hot shower and went to sleep afterward.

The next morning, he arrived at work thirty minutes before time as usual. There was a note attached to his time card. "Don't punch in until I speak with you," signed Hank. Michael was dumbfounded by the note. He went straight to Hank's office. "Come in and close the door behind you Michael," Hand said. Michael looked like he had spooked by a ghost. "Sir is something wrong with my work?" Michael asked. "No this has nothing to do with your work. It's about your personal life." Michael was shocked as hell at Hank's response. "I received a call a few days ago from a police officer named Pearsall. She informed me of your arrest and the charges. I'm sorry to say we have to suspend you without pay. Usually getting arrested would have been grounds to be terminated, but you are a dedicated worker. We will wait for the outcome of the case. I hope you can understand this Michael. You can pick up your last week's paycheck and vacation pay next Tuesday." Hank said. Michal tried to plead with Hank. "Please sir, I need my job. I haven't been convicted of rape, only charges are pending." Michael, there's nothing I can do for you, except hold your position open until we know the outcome of your case," Hank said. Michael sat there slumped over in the chair for a few moments before leaving. He turned in his ID badge.

Michael felt as though his world had crumbled around him. Where in the world was he going to find another job paying him seventy-thousand dollars a year? He went home and he called Metro Police Department to find out how they could ruin someone's life. "Hello, can I speak to Officer Pearsall," Michael asked. The dispatcher checked their computer and could not find an office by that name. "Are you sure?" Michael asked. The dispatcher told Michael no again. Michael slung the phone down with disgust. He pondered over who would call his job, and the first person who crossed his mind was Jackie.

He dialed her number and got her answering machine. He was definitely losing it, the fool left a threatening message. "Yeah, you almost got me fired, bitch. You haven't seen the last of me. My mom always said, "If you lay down with dogs you wake up with fleas". He hung up the phone. Michael had no idea of what he was going to do next. He turned on the television, poured a stiff drink of gin an orange juice. He kept drinking until he was fast asleep.

Chapter 2

It was hard for Roxanne to believe that a month had passed since she joined A.A.M (All About Me). She knew the program required her to speak in front of the group, about her near death experience. This was a healing process from within and every member had to participate. Jackie had never spoken in front of an audience, she was afraid. The counselor told her when she was ready to speak, something inside of her would let her know. Sure enough, it happened just like the counselor told her during her Thursday visit at A.A.M. Roxanne had mustered up the nerves to share her story. "Hi my name is Roxanne, I'm a warrior, not a victim." Her heart was beating fast and her voice cracked a little. Roxanne described how the choices she had made almost cost her, her life when she lived in Liberty City.

"Liberty City wasn't always plagued with drugs and gun violence. My mom often described it as a black haven during the sixties and early seventies. Liberty City was a black community that was filled with hope and happiness. There were all the conveniences at your fingertips, on the main strip of 15 Avenue. The strip glittered with Donut King, Dairy Queen, Bahama Ice Cream Parlor, AMC Movie Theater, House of Albert Funeral Home, Five and Dime Coin

Laundry, Patsy's Beauty Parlor, Kemps Corner Grocery Store, New Hope Church and Liberty Bar. It was a black haven, back in those days. Even the criminals in Liberty City had a code of honor not to rob their own. They would travel to the white areas of Miami and victimize white people. This was the same area they traveled to get some weed or heroin. The white drug pushers didn't trust the blacks to sell cocaine for them, at least not in Miami. Cocaine was a drug for the wealthy.

However, by the mid-seventies, all that changed and I grew up during this era of destructive change. The black man was entrusted to become a seller of cocaine and then crack. Liberty City the community that once looked like hope now looked like a horror flick of the wild-wild-west. A different caliber of black mentality was on the scene. Shootings occurred almost every day, drugs were sold on the street corners like candy and the elderly no longer felt safe sitting on their porch. A community of hope was replaced by a community of fear and chaos.

I dropped out of school at the age of sixteen and by the age of twenty, I had four children. I started smoking marijuana and drinking beer with Derrick my children's father. Derrick left me and got his life together. He moved to another state and became a Police Officer. After he left me and I got involved with another man, who was a cocaine user. It didn't take long before I started using cocaine. In five years' time, I had turned into a strung out "coke" head. Welfare and child support payments helped to finance my drug addiction and these addictions lead me to neglect my children. I never kept enough food in the house to eat and the electricity was turned off every other month. That didn't bother me, I found a way to get some free money from the government emergency funding. All I needed was an eviction notice, and I got plenty of them. I moved around in Liberty City like a gypsy.

My second oldest sister Machell traveling down that same destructive road. Eventually, we moved in together since neither one of us was capable of paying our rent. Also, this gave us more money to give to the drug man. Me and her four children, along with Machell and her three children were all crammed into a two-bedroom apartment. Our rent was only a hundred and fifty dollars a month for rent.

We sold most of our food stamps to Smoky "D", who was our drug supplier. He took full advantage of our addiction and gave us

$235.00 for $600.00 worth of food stamps. In Smoky "D's" eyes he was getting over on the government and his own people, like a "fat rat". Smoky "D" was so good at his drug enterprise that he even cashed welfare checks. He had purchased a corner store in the community. This was his security plan to make sure me, all the other addicts didn't take our welfare money to another drug dealer. As usual, we each brought an eight-ball (cocaine)1 which cost a $100.00, after cashing their checks. Before the night was over we would have made another trip back to Smoky "D".

No matter what our mother, Mattie said to us, we felt no shame. Believe me, she said some hurtful insults that went in one ear and out the other. I know she was trying help and the look in her eyes was that of feeling helpless as a mother, watching us deteriorate. She often brought food over to her grandchildren. Our mother was fifty-five years old, and her health wouldn't allow her to take in all of her grandchildren. However, she got custody of Michelle's oldest daughter Schneika. Schneika was ten years old and was an "a" student.

Our mom kept doing what she could for her other grandchildren. The sight of seeing them in two-day-old pampers filled with shit was sickening. Our apartment was infested with roaches. If you sat down on the couch too long, the roaches would crawl up your leg and welcome you. Once our mom called HRS on us, a lot good that did. HRS made one home visit to us. It just so happened to be on the day we had cleaned up, the kids were clean and there was food in the refrigerator. We told the HRS worker only one us lived in the apartment and the other one was just visiting. Since there weren't any obvious signs of neglect or abuse, nothing was done.

The last week of the month was a critical time for me. My welfare check along with my food stamps was all snorted up my nose. The urge for cocaine would overpower my mind, and this was my cue to walk over to King Red's Lounge and wait for a horny man prospect. My red daisy dukes and blue tank top were my way of giving the signal I was looking for a little action, along with my verbal request, "Hey baby are you looking for a good time, mama can make you feel really good".

The men I usually attract only wanted some head from me. However, this night she thought she had a live bait. This middle height, slender built, average looking white man, with short brown hair, took me up on my offer. Even though it was a little usual for white men, to frequent King Red's Lounge, I didn't give it much thought. Instead of taking me behind the bar like most of the men normally did, he escorted me to his car and what a car it was, a red Infinity. I told him, I hope you don't think you getting the "cookie" on the house tonight, It's going to cost you $25 for thirty minutes." After we pulled out of the parking lot he handed me the $25 dollars and I was smiling all the way to the Smoky "D", anticipating my next "high".

After driving around for about twenty minutes, I asked, where are you taking me? We can get busy right here in the car. The man responded, "I have a special spot just for us". Then he pulled up behind the International Airport, in a secluded area. I thought this man was just another John. Once they got out the car, he ordered me to strip naked. I was humming, "I'm the good thang queen" while undressing. Clueless about what was going to happen. I laid down on the grass with my legs spread eagle in an upward position. Alright, big daddy come over here and give it to me now.

He pulled out a pistol and said, "All right you whacked out bitch, where do you want it, I'm going to put you out of your god damn misery". I jumped up and started pleading for my life, "Please don't kill me, oh Mr., please don't kill me, I have four children". "Yeah, I bet you do, who in the hell would want an ugly motherfucker like you for a mother?" Here take your twenty-five dollars back I don't want your money. "No! It was twenty-five dollars that caused my only son to be dying now," he said.

I found out later that the "John" I had picked up was the "Mad Hooker Killer", who was wanted by the police for the murders of ten hookers. His only son was dying of AIDS after contracting it from a hooker. It was his son's first piece of ass. His son had fallen asleep after his sexual encounter in a cheap motel, only to wake up to a note written across the mirror in red lipstick, "Welcome to the world of AIDS," left there by a deranged hooker.

He continued calling me names, "you are nothing but a two-bit whore". I continued begging for my life and then I fell down to my knees and I began praying like I have never prayed before. "Oh Lord please don't let me die, please don't. I'll change my ways God, just give me another chance please". Just as I uttered the word, please out my mouth, he struck me in the mouth with the handle of the pistol. He became agitated with my praying. He yelled "shut up bitch, as he swung the handle of the pistol against my head until I became unconscious. As I laid on the ground my body motionless, I heard the sound of his car door shut, the engine starts and the car driving away.

He had left me there to die.

God heard my prayers, just as he pulled onto the highway, a police cruiser pulled up behind him. It seemed suspicious for a car to be in that area during the night. They flashed their lights for him to pull over, he did. His hands were covered with blood. The policemen got out with their hands on their revolvers. They ordered him to get out of the car with his hands up. He tried to wipe his hands on his black pants before putting them in the air. Keep your hands in the air, one of the policemen ordered. After examining him and the car, they found traces of blood on his hand and on the handle of his pistol he had shoved under the driver's seat. They put him in the police car for questioning. He told the policemen he had gotten into a fight with a couple of thugs, who tried to rob him and he had gotten lost. His story sounded far-fetched.

They radioed in for a backup unit to go back and check the area they saw him pull off from. The backup unit arrived and after searching the area, they discovered my naked, bloody body. I was still alive. They radioed for an ambulance. The ambulance arrived on the scene I heard the sirens. They rushed me to Jackson Memorial Hospital. My brain was hemorrhaging and my pulse was dropping rapidly. They had to operate fast or I was going to die. The rest of my ordeal was told to me after I recovered. I was put in ICU; I was in a coma. They checked me into the hospital as Jane Doe, because I had Identification on me.

After the police did a ballistic gelatin test on the gun, the test results yield that it was the same gun that was used in the murders of the ten hookers. The police had the Mad Hooker Murder locked up. They needed me to recover because I was the only living witness they had. The six o'clock evening news, ran the story for two days about me title "Jane Doe" and shown a picture of me, hoping someone could identify me.

It wasn't until the second day, my oldest son Cory was watching the news and saw my picture. I was badly beaten, but he was able to recognize me. See this red birthmark in the center of my forehead. Cory started yelling at the top of his lungs. My mama is dead - my mama is dead. He didn't listen to the announcement that followed the picture. He quickly ran next door to use his neighbor's phone. He called my mother, hysterically saying His mama is dead grandma! In between crying, he told her the channel. My mother turned her TV set on and saw nothing. My mother knew the lifestyle I was living, that Jane Doe could possibly be me. She telephoned

Channel 7 Television Station and inquired about a picture they had shown on the air. They gave her the information on what hospital Jane Doe was at. My mom drove to the hospital hoping all the way there that it wasn't me. It wasn't unusual for me not to come home for days at a time, therefore my sister Machell wasn't alarmed when I didn't come home.

My mom arrived at Jackson Memorial Hospital in a state of panic. The nurse at the information station had someone take her in to see Jane Doe in I.C.U. The sight of my beat up face and tubes running out of my mouth, nearly caused my mother to faint. She had to catch her balance by holding on to the wall. She walked over slowly to the side of my bed. Unstoppable tears rolled down her face. "Why, Lord, Why Roxanne"? my mom asked aloud. Then she held my right hand and squeezed it tight. Hoping I would open my eyes. I showed no signs of movement. My mother sat down in the chair and waited for the doctor to give her an update on my condition.

Meanwhile, the nurse at the information station followed the instructions left by the policeman. If anyone identified Jane Doe, contact Detective. Watson at Metro Dade Police Department immediately. After receiving the call, Detective Watson arrived at the

hospital in no time. He entered my room and spoke to my mother."
He introduced himself to my mom. He knew that it wasn't the best
time to talk to her; however, he was assigned to my case. My mother
stared at him with blankness She asked Detective Watson did they
have the sick son of a bitch who did this to her daughter? He told my
mom yes. They caught him leaving the scene. He was also wanted for
ten other murders in which we only have circumstantial evidence.
Detective Watson told my mother I was the only living witness, they
had. If I pulled through, it's vital that he be contacted immediately.
My mother shook her head nodding yes.

My mom called my sister Michelle's neighbor to relay a
message to my son Corey, that I wasn't dead. Corey demanded to
come to the hospital to be with me. He was a bright and loving five-
year-old. Machell was emotionally frozen after our mother told her
about my condition. My mother called her other 7 adult children and
told them what had happened to me. Three of my brothers and my
oldest sister Cynthia brought Corey to the hospital.

Cynthia led my siblings in a prayer for my recovery. This sight
of them praying was comforting for our mother. The hospital policy
didn't allow children of Corey's age to go into an ICU patient's room,

but they made an exception for him after he put on a scene of crying. He stood next to his mother's bed and cried repeatedly, mumbling the same words "mama don't leave us, we need you and we love you". When visiting hours were over, Corey refused to leave. After all the commotion, they decided to let him. He stayed the night, along with his grandmother by my bedside.

The next morning Corey woke up and started whispering "Mama I love you in my ear, and he remembered a nursery rhyme I use to sing to him. It was something I made up once. "I am the sunshine and you are the plant. I will shower you with love to help you grow". The sound of those words caused some movement in my hand. Corey repeated the nursery rhyme again and my eyelids opened. "Mama, Mama I knew you wouldn't leave us, oh mama", he screamed.

My mom was in the hallway, sitting in the brown chair she had slept in the night before. At the sound of Corey's voice, she ran into the room and saw a beautiful sight. Her daughter was alive. "Thank you, Lord, "she yelled". Then she bent over and kissed me on the cheek. The nurse came into the room to examine me and was shocked to see my eyes open, however, I couldn't see out of one of them. The doctor was summoned to my room. The doctor stated it was a sheer miracle that I was alive. However, I had a long road of therapy ahead of me. The left and right part of my brain hemisphere was slightly damaged and would require therapy. Detective. Watson was called to come to the hospital.

Once he arrived, he knew this wasn't the best time to ask any question, but they needed to charge the Mad Hooker Killer with attempted murder charges on me. He brought in a 6 picture photo line-up for me to look at. Detective Watson told me to blink my eyes if she could Identify the man who nearly beat me to death. He showed me the line-up and when I looked at the Mad Hooker Murder the expression on my face told the story. Detective Watson pointed to his picture and I blinked my eyes. Tears started running down my face, my mom wiped them away with her hand.

After everyone left my room, I started thinking about the sound of Corey's voice and how he begged me not to die. If that wasn't enough to make me straighten up my life, then I don't know what would be. I closed my eyes and began praying silently to God. I asked God to strengthen me with the willpower to overcome this drug addiction and to help me create a new beginning in life.

They charged Charles Zerlin, aka the Mad Hooker Killer, with the attempted murder of me After Detective Watson told him I had identified him, he confessed to all 10 murders.

Two weeks after my ordeal, I began my therapy. Denard Johnson was my therapist. He worked on my speech and the use of my hands and feet. I felt comfortable with him. He always told me jokes and complimented me on my inner and outer beauty, even though I had to have my right eye removed and replaced with a glass eye. The damage from the pistol had destroyed all the nerves in it. Some of the deceased victim's family sent me flowers, thank you and get-well cards for helping with the conviction of Mr. Zerlin aka The Mad Hooker Killer. To them, I was their hero, allowing them to close a chapter in their lives.

After six months of therapy, Denard had fallen in love with me and he knew he had to get me out of Liberty City. A week before I was discharged; he told me how he felt about me. My face lit up like a Christmas tree. He also told me of his plan to move back to his home-town, Pie County. He wanted me and my children to move with him. I said yes and asked how soon could we leave. Denard had already put in for a tentative transfer to the Pie County General Hospital. Moving to Pie County worked out great, my cousin Janice and her mother, Pearl lives here.

My mother, Mattie was very happy for me; I was getting a second chance to do something good with my life. As soon as I took care of all my personal business and got the children's school transfer paperwork, we packed up everything and rented a U-Haul truck and drove to Pie County the week after I was released. Once I got settled in Pie County, I contacted my cousin Janice and we made plans to meet the following week. Janice was overwhelmed to see me it had been years since we last saw each other.

Once I told Janice a few details of what I had gone through she recommended that I joined A.A.M. She was right, my self-esteem was in the gutter and it needed a boost. Here I am a month later at A.A.M. and sharing my ordeal. Now I'm on the path to healing. Thank you all for listing." She received a standing ovation from the women in attendance. The women came up and gave her a group hug. It was hard for Roxanne to fight back the tears, that rolled down her face, these were tears of joy, not pain. Roxanne had never felt so relieved after sharing her ordeal, it felt like a rock had been lifted off her back.

Denard didn't know how emotionally, spiritually or mentally

Roxanne had been scared throughout her life. However, he willing to get her whatever help she needed. He registered her in an outpatient drug treatment center the second week after their arrival in Pie County. It was a unique drug treatment center called D.A.M. - (Drug-Addicted-Mothers). Dr. Wilkson was the director of the center. He devoted most of his time to it. He was a warm, caring and knowledgeable doctor. He had a personal interest in D.A.M. During his last year of medical school at Washington University, his mother overdosed on heroin. He felt compelled to make a difference in the lives of women who were addicted to drugs. After attending these sessions three times a week, Roxanne understood how her drug addiction had a severe impact on her children and family lives.

The first step at D.A.M. is to accept responsibility for becoming a drug addict. The second step is to apologize to your family members. These are the people you hurt the most. Roxanne, went home and called her mother on the telephone and begin crying and she apologized. Roxanne's mother knew by the sound of her voice that she was sincere and on her way to recovery. All her mother could do on the other end of the phone is shout "thank you, Jesus, thank you, Jesus, oh how good God is". Then she told Roxanne I love you and I'm here if you need me. Roxanne told her mother she loved her too and thanks for standing in her corner when no one else would and hung up the telephone.

When her children arrived home from school, she sat them down. Corey immediately asked was something wrong. She told him no, I just need to speak with you all. She started the conversation off by saying how much she loved each one of them. They were all old enough to know that she was a drug addict. Their ages ranged from 12, 11,10 and 6 years old. She continued with her conversation, she said I'll never know how much I hurt you by using drugs but I want to say I'm sorry. There is no excuse for using drugs. My love for you all should have been greater than my love for drugs. Can you all ever forgive me?

Her children sat next to her and threw their arms around her and said, mommy, we love you and forgive you. Tears running down all of their little faces and snot dripping from their nose. That was a divine moment in Roxanne's life. The feeling, she felt for her children is unexplainable, but it felt good. She continued taking small steps to make a positive change in their lives. She joined the PTA and got involved with their homework and set aside one weekend a month for her children. Roxanne's progress was great, her sessions at DAM was reduced to once a week. There was still one area, she needed help in, that was finding a way to share herself sexually with Denard.

Denard knew it was going to take some time before Roxanne became intimately involved with him. However, he had no idea how long it would be. It was a month after they moved to Pie County before he even tried to touch her romantically in bed. She freaked out and started accusing him of taking advantage of her body. He jumped out of the bed and told her to calm down. He would go sleep on the couch. Sleeping on the couch became a routine for the next few weeks.

During one of the sessions at A.A.M., Janice brought up the subject of her not being able to get sexually involved with Denard. She loved him, but she didn't want him to touch her sexually. The truth be told, Denard was the first man, who loved her for her mind and not her body.

Girtrue was one of the senior counselors at A.A.M., she responded to Roxanne statement. She told Roxanne to close her eyes and imagine that she was at a beach." Listen to the sound of the ocean waves. Take a deep breath in and release it. Concentrate on your breathing. She told her to repeat this exercise twice. Don't open your eyes, do you love yourself, Roxanne?" She asked. "Of course I do." Roxanne responded Girtrue asked her the next question, "Do you think you are worthy to be loved by Denard?" Roxanne didn't respond. Girtrue continued talking, "If you love yourself, the answer should have been yes quickly. Denard is none of the men who have hurt you in the past. He has proven that he loves you, by relocating you and your children to Pie County without ever sleeping with you. He doesn't even know if you are good in bed." The other ladies made a gasping sound when Girtrue said that. Girtrue continued, "You don't know too many men, not even my husband would have taken a gamble like Denard has. He loves you, Roxanne. You should make the next move, to let him know you love him too." Girtrue told Roxanne to open her eyes and a big smile came on her face.

She hugged Girtrue and thanked her for sharing those words of enlightenment. Girtrue told her she was welcome. Girtrue also recommended that Roxanne takes her children to counseling. Girtrue had seen too many women, who were drug addicts, get themselves together and think their kids are ok. What they fail to realize is, their children are the collateral damage from their addiction. Roxanne agreed to take her children to get counseling, she didn't want them to make the same bad choices she did. Roxanne left the sessions, realizing how grateful she was to have a man in her life like Denard.

She finally realized why it was hard for her to get sexually involved with Denard. She had not forgiven herself, for the choices she had made in life. Somewhere along her journey, she had stopped loving herself without realizing it.

Roxanne arrived home after her A.A.M. meeting, she went into the bathroom and stared at herself in the mirror. She recited the motto from the A.A.M. meeting; "God only created one of you, you are special no matter what choices you've made in life. You can't change the past, for the past was a classroom from which you've learned from. You have to move from believing to knowing, that you have the ability to create your own destiny. I love you." Tears of joy rolled down her face as she let out a loud gasping sound of relief.

Roxanne made arrangements for her children to stay the night at Janice's house. She cooked a nice meal. Then she showed and slipped into her hot pink negligee and lit some candles. Denard had kept a bottle of Champaign in the refrigerator for a special occasion. Roxanne figure it was time to take the bottle out.

When Denard came into the house, he noticed the children

were missing He went upstairs to their bedroom. Roxanne was stretched out on the bed in her hot pink negligee with Smokey Robinson was crooning "Baby Come Close" was in the CD player. Denard loved "old school" music. Denard smiled as if he had just hit the lotto. He took off his work clothes and showered quickly. Then they sipped on Champaign and she disclosed her fears to him. They both agreed to take one day at a time in bed. They caressed at first, then he kissed her body gently and sucked on her toes. They made love like they were high school teenagers. Every emotion felt anew and every feeling was an ecstasy. This was a feeling worth waiting for, Denard thought to himself. When they finish making love, they fell asleep in each other's arms.

The next morning the alarm clock went off. Denard kissed Roxanne on the forehead and then the lips. She rolled over on top him and they started kissing passionately. He said alright don't start anything you can't finish. Roxanne jokingly said give me ten minutes and I will show you what I can finish. Denard didn't put a fight and they made love. It was hard for Denard to go to work afterward but he did.

Roxanne had enrolled in night school and earned her GED. She also took some clerical and computer courses, that helped her get a job that was fifteen minutes away from where she lived in uptown. It has been three years since Denard moved Roxanne and the kids from Liberty City and they are making plans to get married.

Chapter 3

Peter was the type of man most women regret not marrying, especially after they had a taste of a man with the "fire". This premature emotion called the "fire" causes an uncontrollable lust in some women and men, which leads them to confuse lust for love. In the end, they are sexually fulfilled and emotionally drained.

Peter was slender built, no biceps anywhere, a low haircut and stood about 5'7. He had a deep baritone voice, and well versed. He could hold a discussion about anything. He finished college and his doctrine education. He worked as a principal at Pie County Alternative School, for teenage boys who got expelled from public school.

Peter was five years older than Janice, who was twenty-seven. When Janice first met Peter at Hope's Supermarket in the frozen food section, he took her shopping cart by mistake. He realized this before he got to the end of the aisle when he saw panty-hose in the shopping cart. He quickly turned the cart around and took it back to Janice, who standing in the middle of the aisle with her hand on her hip. "Excuse me miss, is this your shopping cart," he asked. Janice put a half smile on her face and said yes. He apologized graciously for the honest mistake. He was so embarrassed by the whole mix up that he invited her for a cup of coffee at Tilquanda's Heavenly Deli, located next door.

Taking her shopping cart was not a good first impression to Janice, however, out of curiosity she had a cup of coffee and a sandwich, with him anyway. Janice was checking him out from top to the bottom, listening to every word he uttered. He had a perfect set of teeth that gleamed every time he smiled. After they small talked for about forty-five minutes he asked her for her phone number. She gave it to him and as she walked away, she wondered why she gave it to him. He wasn't her type, she was used to dating men who appeared to be rough edges, with tattoos on their arms. Peter didn't appear to possess that take charge attitude, that Janice was used to having in a man. He appeared to be too laid back for her.

A week later Petered called Janice and invited her to go see a play. The play titled "God Please Send Me A Man", Sharon and Marshea were the producers of the play, they were a dynamite mother and daughter team, out of Atlanta GA.

They went to see the play and Angela was the main characters in the play, who kept dating the wrong type of men. She didn't give God any particular description as to what type of man she wanted.

Angela realized towards the end of the play, that she had to be very detailed when asking God to send a man into her life. She prayed to God, to send her a man, who could love her, treat her with respect, wasn't violent, had a job and wanted more out of life. While in the shower, the voice of God spoke to her and said, before she could meet that man she had to make changes within herself. Angela knew exactly what the voice of God was talking about. She had to change her mindset, and let go of the negative luggage she had been carrying around. God answered her prayers, she met Junior and a later they got married, the end. The audience stood up and clapped.

Peter and Janice both enjoyed the play and afterward, they went to have a scoop of French vanilla ice cream. As they drove home, she thought the play was appropriate for her. In her mind, she believed that God had sent her two men. In the passing months, Peter had fallen in love with Janice. They never argued, they agreed to disagree like two mature adults. Peter knew how important effective communication is in any relationship. He didn't allow his ego or pride to govern his love for Janice. These characteristics stood out in Janice's mind along with his sureness of who he was as a black man. He encouraged her to pursue whatever, she was interested in.

Janice was a beautiful woman, but her self-esteem had taken a beaten from past relationships, including the one she had with the first man who loved her, her father. Her father had no idea of the impact his negative words would have on her as an adult. Her father wanted the best for her, but he didn't have the mental or emotional capacity to give it to her. He used the only tools, he had grown-up with, which was "negativity" disguised as love. This was something Peter had observed, every time she discussed ideas about starting her own business. She would mention to him how her father had told her she wouldn't amount to anything without an education. She would have to sell her body to make a living. Although she struggled in high school, she did finish.

She didn't believe she had the ability to start her own business. Peter would whisper in her ear, "baby you can do anything, I believe in you". Janice would smile and give him a kiss on the cheek and say thank you. She wanted to believe every word he said, however, she couldn't wrap her mind around it. She dated Peter for eight months before circumstances left her relying on the love he had for her. During this eight-month period, Janice was still dating Kevin. She had been dating Kevin for a year before she met Peter. Kevin had that so-called "fire" of desire, and he was using Janice with it.

Kevin was about 6"3, with a dark cocoa complexion and sported a six-pack that would make you lose your breath just by looking at him. His biceps peeped out from his t-shirt and those candy licking lips were sexy as hell. If he got paid for his looks and charisma, hell he could have been a male model and rich. Instead, Kevin used his good looks to lure women into his world, used them and dump them. The brother had skills. He was a smooth talker, he told the women just want they needed to hear and made them believe he was the man of their dreams.

Kevin had three children and he wasn't doing a damn thing for any of them. If it weren't for the Pie County's State Attorney 's Office, Child Support Enforcement Unit his children wouldn't get a dime from his sorry ass. He manipulated Janice into paying his child support payments that were in the arrears. Like a fool, she was paying them with the hard-earned money she had saved for a rainy day. It was used for a rainy day alright, in the form of a fool in love.

After they made love, Kevin would run the same sad ass love story to her. "You're the best woman I ever dated. One-day baby when we get married, I'll make it up to you." Like an idiot, Janice bought all those rehearsed lines, until one day when the shit hit the fan.

Janice went over to Kevin's house unannounced at 9 a.m. He had given her a key to his duplex, to fool her into believing she was the only woman in his life. Out of respect for him, she always called to let him know she was coming over, however, this day her woman's intuition told her to just pop up over there. Once she arrived, she saw a baby blue Toyota parked in Kevin's driveway. Janice became suspicious because the tag in the front of the car had "Sexy Red ", on it.

Janice knew Kevin's next door neighbor was out of town, therefore she parked in their driveway. She went around to Kevin's back door, the same key unlocked the front and back doors. She slipped inside the house without making a sound. She stood in the kitchen as she heard loud laughter coming from the master bedroom. One of the voices she recognized as Kevin, the other one was a woman. She had to grasp for air, before tiptoeing to the bedroom door to listen for a while. She had no idea of what she was about to hear.

Kevin "low rating" her in the worst possible way. He said, "I've been talking to this dumb chick named Janice. Monique baby, when God made her, He broke the dumb mold. shit, she paid most of my child support arrears, I was able to put your thousand-dollar diamond engagement ring on layaway at Diamonds by Crystal and she is going to give me the money to renew my car insurance. She thinks I'm going to marry her cause I tapped that ass really good, she thinks I'm in love with her. Those sized triple D titties of hers are so damn ugly I have to close my eyes whenever I fuck her." Monique laughed so hard until she started crying

Janice was frozen stiff she had never felt so humiliated in all of her life. Sure, she had large breast, however, that's a body feature that runs on her mother's side of the family. She had a small waistline and a plump ass that complemented her figure.

The bedroom door was cracked open, allowing her to peeped in the room without either one of them noticing her. She wanted to see want the hell did Monique looked like. They were too busy kissing to see her staring at them through the cracked door. Monique was a red-boned female, well portioned in her all body parts except her breast. Hell her breast was just as big as. Janice.

Janice quietly stepped back from the door and leaned against the wall in the hallway. She felt a rush of anger go through her body.

She made her way to the living room and stared at the rifle hanging over his fake fireplace. She wanted to snatch the rifle off the rack and blow their god damn brains out. Kevin had always kept bullets in the rifle. For a few moments, she entertained that thought. She couldn't think straight; her heart was racing at the pace of a thorough-bred reaching the finish line.

Then she snapped back to reality and realized they weren't worth her going to prison for. Suppose the bullets didn't kill them? They would still be on the outside doing the same thing and she would be locked up behind bars. The sound of Kevin's loud groaning and Monique yelling out, give it to me baby, coming from the bedroom made Janice sick to her stomach. She slipped out the back door, closing it with ease.

Janice drove around for an hour in a daze. While stopped at a red light on Main Avenue she saw a derelict washing his body in a polluted river. Her life didn't seem so out of control after that scene, but the pain didn't go away. She couldn't stop crying. She stopped at a corner store to call Peter. She needed to hear the sound of his mellow voice more than anything now. But he wasn't at home.

Then she drove back to her apartment and sat idle, in one spot staring at the walls, until a knock on the door got her attention. "Who is it?" she asked. "It's your Aunt Lucy, honey." Aunt Lucy was her mother's second oldest sister. "Just a minute Aunt Lucy" Janice wiped her eyes dry before opening the door. Aunt Lucy had that "old school mentality", she was fifty- nine. Her Aunt Lucy didn't believe a woman should cry over a man. Aunt Lucy was a pro at getting even with a son of a bitch who cheats. She believed that you should reap whatever seeds you sow when it comes to love. Janice opened the door and tried to put on a phony smile, but Aunt Lucy saw straight through that bullshit-smile. Janice's eyes were bloodshot red from crying.

Girl, I know you haven't been crying over no man. You know I don't play that shit." "No," said Janice. "Then what the hell have you been crying for?" Aunt Lucy asked. Janice couldn't think of a quick lie to say. She broke down and told her what happened at Kevin's house. "Girl, didn't I teach you anything when you were living with me? You don't give a man a dime unless he has given you a dollar." "Aunt Lucy for the first time in my life I wanted to kill someone," said Janice. "No baby, you don't kill a man, you get even." "How can I get even Aunt "Lucy." "He still expects you to pay his last three child support payments and his down payment for his insurance?" "Yeah." "Ok, then we have some shit to work with honey."

She told Janice about one of her get even with a man stories from her younger days. "His name was Charlie, girl the man was breaking me off those funds and he could slang that dick in bed. That sneaky bastard lied to me about not being married. He had given me his mother's phone number instead of his number. He told me he was taking care of his mother because she had heart surgery. It took me a little time before I noticed a pattern, every time I called he was never there. However, he always returned my calls within ten minutes.

One night after we had dinner and he dropped me off home, I got in my car and followed his ass. Just as I suspected, the address he gave me for his home address was not the same one he entered. He must have given me one of his relative's addresses for his own or a fake one. I did not play that shit. I started to knock on his got damn, door and start some shit that night but I didn't. He had broken my motherfucking motto, "come clean with your shit or don't come at all. Hell if he would have been honest up front, I might have still kicked it with his ass.

The next morning, I drove to the house that I had watched Charlie go into the night before. I had borrowed my friend girl's green

Honda Accord to make sure I didn't get caught. I was parked a few houses down. Charlie came out the door, got into his Red Chevy Pick-up truck and drove off. Once he was out sight, I drove in front of the two-story house, got out the car, and knocked on the door. I didn't know what to expect but I ready if any shit jumped off. Like American Express, baby I never leave home without my switchblade.

A woman opened the door. She was a beautiful woman, I don't why in the hell Charlie was stepping out on her. She appeared to be a few years older than I was but she younger than Charlie. Nevertheless, I was wearing my hot red backless dress that is cut low in the front, so the family jewels were peeping out at her, my red pumps and my red lipstick to match. I asked was Charlie home, the woman said no, but could she help me with something, because she was Charlie's wife, Diane. I said, yes you certainly can. I told her I was Charlie's girlfriend and Charlie told me he wasn't married. The expression on Diane's face was a candid camera moment. She stared me down from head to toe. Then she said, excused me, you are who? I knew the bitch heard me the first time but since I had no beef with her I repeated, his girlfriend. I told her I wasn't there to start no shit with her, I was there to put an end to Charlie cheating ass.

She asked the usual stupid questions, how long we've been dating, where did we meet, etc. I told her none of that mattered, just let me come in and call Charlie at work. She could listen to our conversation to prove what I was saying was the truth. Diane was a little reluctant, but she wanted to get to the bottom of this shit. She had noticed for the past five months, that Charlie had been claiming he was working late on Fridays and Saturdays. Charlie was the owner of an auto repair shop. He was a mechanic as well and working late wasn't usual, but it was a little suspect that those were the only days he worked late.

I called Charlie and told him that one of my girlfriends said he married. Charlie denied being married and in a reassuring tone called me sweetheart. He went on to profess that I was the only woman for him. To prove his point to me he said he would confront this so-called friend of mine. I told Charlie, I would bring my friend to his business so he can straighten this mess out. Charlie agreed. Before hanging up the phone he asked me to wear that red dress with the back out and the split up the side. Hell, that was the dress I was wearing.

Diane was mad as hell and it took everything in her to keep from cussing that son of a bitch. out. She knew she had his no good ass by the balls. She was casually dressed, wearing a pair of blue jeans and a yellow tank top. She couldn't wait to see his god damn face. We arrived at Charlie's business in twenty minutes. I went in first and laid down the loving foundation with Charlie. He greeted me with a smile and planted a big sloppy kiss on my lips as he gently squeezed my juicy ass.

Before he could look up, Diane was standing in the doorway. He jumped back and wanted to know what kind of bullshit was this. Diane walked up to him and slapped the shit out of his face. She hit him so hard until the bones in her fingers felt as though they were broken. Then I sucker slapped the other side of his face. My last words to Charlie were, how low can a man get, you have a wife and you're still trying to put a lock on my vibrant pussy. I never heard from Charlie again and don't know if he was able to patch things up with Diane. Now the man I'm dating now has his shit together, I'm too old to be playing games."

Janice felt a lot better after hearing Aunt Lucy's get even man's story. Aunt Lucy told Janice to go ahead and give Kevin the money for his back child support payments and his insurance. Are you crazy Aunt Lucy? I'm not giving his sorry ass any more of my damn money." Janice said. "Honey, I didn't say he was actually going to benefit from your money. I'll guarantee you Kevin will never forget you after this shit goes down," said Aunt Lucy.

Aunt Lucy told Janice to give him the money in the form of checks, sign her signature differently, fill in the amounts and leave the dates and the payee blank. Once she gave Kevin the checks, wait an hour, then go to the bank and report her checks stolen. "Call me, once you've reported your checks stolen and leave the rest to me," said Aunt Lucy.

Janice wanted to know how soon should she put the plan into action. Aunt Lucy told her the sooner the better. As soon as Aunt Lucy left, it took everything in Janice to call Kevin and get the ball rolling. "Hello, Kevin how are you doing?" "Fine baby and yourself?" "Oh, I'm doing great. I was just calling to let you know I cashed my CD's (certificates of deposits) from my credit union at my bank. So I'll have to write checks for your child support payments and your car insurance." In a condescending voice, Kevin asked why she couldn't give him cash. She told him that her bank had a two-day hold on the funds from the CD's and by the time the checks got to her back the cash will be available.

Janice's voice began to crack a little as tears begin to roll down her face. She told Kevin to hold on for a minute. She had to compose herself. She returned to the phone and told him the sooner he had his affairs in order, they could start making wedding plans. Kevin agreed. "I'll be over there in 30 minutes to drop the checks off. "Come on by, I can't wait to see you, sweetheart," said Kevin. "I bet you can't," said Janice as she hung up the phone.

After Kevin hung up the phone, he told Monique she had to leave so he could get the money from Janice. However, he was going to dump her after he made his payments with her checks. Monique got up, put on her clothes and left. Kevin took a quick shower and put clean sheets on his bed.

Janice arrived at Kevin's house like clockwork, within 30 minutes. He was all smiles and hugs. "Come on in baby, can I get you something to drink." "Oh no, I'm not thirsty. Here are the checks, I filled in the amounts and signed them. I wasn't sure of the exact names of the payee, so I left them and the dates blank." Kevin was happy to get those checks in his hand. He had no problem with the information being left blank on the checks. He would fill them in. He kissed Janice on the cheek and her body went numb as hell. It took everything she had in her body to keep from spitting in that bastard's face. She kept her composure. As she was leaving Kevin told her would stop by her house later. She put on a fake smile as replied ok. Janice got into her car and drove off in a hurry.

Janice went by Junior's Jamaican All Beef Burger joint and grabbed a bite to eat to pass the time. Her bank didn't close until 7 pm. When she finished eating, she went to the bank and reported her checks stolen and closed out her account. Once she reached her home, she phoned Aunt Lucy and told her that she had done her part of the plan. No sooner had Janice left out the door, Kevin put on a pair of blue jeans and a t-shirt and headed to A.R. Insurance Company. Kevin was a regular customer, so accepting Janice's check was no problem. He gave the insurance agent the check for the down payment for his car insurance. He drove to the Pie County's State Attorney's Office to make his child support payments.

Kevin was happy like a frog on a log. Then he drove by Janice's apartment to dump her. Kevin knocked on Janice's door. She opened the door and ushered for him to come in. He came in. Janice told him to have a seat, he told her he wasn't staying long. "Janice our relationship is going to work out, it's over." Janice asked him calmly, "Are you sure this is what you want to do Kevin? What about all the money I've given you?" Kevin responded, "Look at the money you've given me as an expensive investment in love baby. You don't think I was really going to marry a girl like you?" "Get the hell out! You no good motherfucker!" "Alright I'm going, but give me my door keys because you won't be using them anymore," said Kevin. Janice threw the keys in his face, hoping they would hit the shit out of him, unfortunately, he caught them in time. He left. Janice leaned against the door, she wanted to cry but the tears wouldn't come down. She

Aunt Lucy had already contacted her friend Thomas, who was a detective at the Pie County Police Department about Janice's stolen checks and told him where he could start his investigation. Thomas was a longtime friend of Aunt Lucy's. They once dated, in her younger days, but it didn't work out. The love they had for each other, allowed them to remain good friends over the years. When Thomas got married Aunt Lucy attended his wedding.

The next day Detective Thomas Brunson went to A.R. Insurance Company. The insurance agent checked the log of payments received and there it was, big as daylight, a payment from Kevin Hudson with Janice's check. The insurance agent had already sent the company's check into Casualty Insurance but a phone call would cancel Kevin's policy. Janice's check had not yet been deposited and Detective Thomas Brunson took it in for evidence. Detective Brunson went to the child support depository and again there was Janice's other check. Kevin had signed documents at both places where he issued Janice's checks. Detective Brunson took copies of the documents and the checks back to their handwriting lab and the handwriting expert examine them. Kevin's handwriting on the payee of the checks matched the handwriting on the documents he had signed at the insurance company and the child support depository.

Kevin was back at his house enjoying Monique's luscious body once again. They were celebrating his conquest of another one of his women victims. Kevin had a habit of using women, getting what he wanted and then kicking them to the curve. Monique was his main girlfriend and she always reaped the benefits he took from other women.

The handwriting report came back, as a match, Detective Brunson contacted the Criminal Intake Unit at the Pie County's State Attorney's Office to make sure he had enough to make an arrest. One of the Chief, Assistant State Attorney's Marie Jo, who gave him the green light to make the arrest.

Aunt Lucy made a special request for the timing of Kevin's arrest. She told Detective Brunson to go and pick him up around 11 p.m. She knew he would be in bed with some woman. Detective Brunson arrived at Kevin's house around 11 p.m. Kevin was laying in the bed with Monique. They had just finished screwing when a hard knock on the door puzzled Kevin and Monique. Kevin thought it was Janice at first, but he knew she wouldn't have balls enough to do some shit like this. He got up and went to the door in his boxer shorts and peeped through the door hole. Detective Brunson put his badge up to the hole. Kevin quickly opened the door, "Can I help you?" "Are you Kevin Hudson?" "Yes, I am." "I have a warrant for your arrest for uttering stolen checks." "Nah you got me all wrong. I haven't issued any stolen checks." "We can do this the easy way or the hard way. Put your pants and shirt on and come with me." Kevin put on his pants and shirt in a hurry. Detective Brunson put the handcuffs on Kevin.

"Monique I need you to follow us to the jail, so you can bail me out." Monique asked, "with what?" "Come on girl don't play games with me." "Hell I'm not playing games, I'm not one of those use me for my money women". "Fuck it, just get the receipt out my top drawer and go to Diamonds by Crystal and get the money I had put down on your damn ring." "All right young man, that's enough of all that talking," said Detective Brunson as he escorted Kevin outside, and put into the police car. Detective Brunson booked Kevin into Pie County Jail.

The next morning Monique took the receipt to Diamonds by Crystal but she couldn't get the $400.00 deposit that Kevin had put down on her ring. Only Kevin could get the deposit back.

Peter came over to Janice's house that night. Janice cried like a baby in his arms. She told him in so many words about Kevin and what had happened between the two. She didn't know if Peter was going to walk out on her, but she owed him that much. He took her in his arms and told her to look into his eye. He wanted to her on

a journey of love. As he stared back into her eyes and his lips whispered. "I understand how easy it is to get involved with the wrong person. I kind of had an idea you were seeing someone else but the love I have for you allowed me to patiently wait for you to figure out which one of us you wanted. I forgive you, I want to take you to my private island, where you are my queen and I'm your king. I will spend every day finding new ways to put a smile on your face. He reached forward and sealed his love for her with a passionate kiss on her lips. Janice hugged him so tight, she didn't want to let go.

Then they lay back on the couch, he slowly unbuttoned her shirt and caressed her breast with his hands. He removed her red panties and begin massaging her clitoris gently with his fingertips. Then they made hot passionate love for the first time. She was breathing heavy from every touch of Peter's hand all over her body. Once he was inside of her, she moaned with the sound of satisfaction. Then he began groaning with every stroke Janice made. As he came down she went up. Afterwards, they both collapsed and went to sleep in each other's arms.

Meanwhile, Kevin was sitting in jail hoping that Monique would get the money and bail him out. He laid down on the hard iron cot, thinking about who could have done this to him. At first, he thought it was his twin brother Kevon. He thought Kevon was using his name again. Kevin hustled women, Kevon was a hustler in the street. Kevon had been in and out jail since he was 18 years old. Kevin had never been arrested in his life. He was clueless.

The victim's name on the A-form listed Janice Cox as the

victim. He was dumbfounded, how could she do something like this to him. When he got home, he called her and got a recording stating the number he had dialed has been changed to an unlisted number. He decided to go over there to whip some sense into her dumb head.

Peter had left's Janice apartment at 6 a.m. to go to work. Once he got over there, he banged on the door. Janice didn't answer the door. She continued sitting on her brown love seat listening to him ranting outside her door. He said, "I know you're in there I need to talk to you."

Janice called the police and told them someone was trying to break into her apartment. The police substation was down the street from her apartment complex. The police were dispatched within minutes. Before Kevin knew what she had done the police cars had pulled in front of her apartment complex. They walked up to Kevin and one of the officer's asked, "All right sir let's put l your hands in the air." Kevin knew his luck couldn't be this damn bad. He just got out of jail. "I haven't done anything wrong", Kevin said. The officer told him they got a call that someone was trying to break into the apartment you are standing in front of and you match the description that was given to the dispatcher. "No sir, you got it all wrong, I know the lady that lives here. I just want to talk to her."

Janice opened her door and told the officer she had nothing to say to Kevin and that she filed a criminal complaint against him for stealing her checks. The police officer ran Kevin's name through their computer system. It revealed that he had been arrested for grand theft and uttering two forged instruments and Janice was listed as the victim. The police officer told Kevin he had to leave and not to return or he was going to jail. They advised Janice to get a restraining order.

As Kevin started to leave, he begged Janice not to do this to him. Janice asked the officer could she say one thing to him? The officer said yes. She whispered in his ear, "Let this be a lesson to you, be careful who you fuck over because the price you will have to pay won't equal the pain you caused. If you make restitution, give me an extra $500.00 for my pain, I will try to drop the charges." Kevin went home looking like a dog with its tail between his legs.

For the first time in his life, taking advantage of a woman backfired on his ass. He looked around his house for anything pawn-able. He called Monique to find out what happened to the money from the ring. She told him that the deposit could only be refunded to him.

He asked, "so you couldn't come up with any bail money?"

Monique responded, "I don't give my money to men, they give me theirs." He was pissed off by that statement and cursed Monique out. "Whore if it wasn't for you, I wouldn't be in this situation in the first place. You're nothing but a got damn user," said Kevin. "Yeah that's me the queen of users and I've used the hell out of you. See you around town sucker, you've just been licked." Those were the last words Monique said as she hung up the phone.

Kevin took his bowling ball, his lawn mower, his rifle and Rolex watch that he had gotten from one of the well-to-do women that his male ego had victimized. He drove to the Bob's Pawn Shop and got the money and went to Diamond's by Crystal and got his deposit back minus $25.00. He drove back over to Janice house and knocked her door like a man with some sense. He told her he had $1800.00 dollars to give her. Janice told him to slip the money through the mail slot. He put the money in the mail slot. "Janice are you going to get the charges dropped" Kevin asked. Janice responded, "I'll see what I can do". Kevin left and went home. He still couldn't believe the shit, Janice pulled on him. She didn't seem like she would have the brains to pull something like that. Kevin thought to himself. Janice called her Aunt Lucy and told her she had gotten her money back from Kevin.

Aunt Lucy informed Janice that if she didn't show-up for the pre-file conference the case would most likely be dropped. Detective Brunson wasn't going to show either.

A few weeks had passed since her horrible ordeal with Kevin. Janice nor Detective Brunson showed up for their pre-file conferences and the charges were eventually dropped. She never heard from Kevin again. She was thankful to God for miracles, like Peter. Their relationship was moving in the right directions and he never brought up the incident with Kevin.

One morning while Janice was getting ready for work the phone rang and it was Karen, Jackie's sister. She called to let her know that one of the hottest comedians was coming to Pie County to perform next week. She asked Janice to purchase the tickets at Muffie's Boutique and Crazy Things located in the shopping mall across from her job. During Janice's lunch-

break, she went across the street to the mall to purchase the tickets. However, Muffie's Boutique and Crazy Things were sold out.

Janice saw Roxanne eating a sandwich at "John's and Walnisha, All You Eat Sub Shop," and walked over and joined her. "What's up Roxanne? She responded, nothing much. "So what's been happening with you? I haven't heard from you in a minute?" Janice responded, "I'm doing great now, but if you had asked me a few weeks ago honey, my story had a sad ending." "What happened?" "I found out first hand that Kevin was using me for my money. "So what between you and happen?" "Honey, the man played me like a blank CD. But that's alright, I started out as a blank CD but in the end, he was singing, "It's a thin line between love and hate," thanks to my Aunt Lucy." They both fell out laughing. "Now I'm in a meaningful and happier relationship with Peter". Said Janice "Say what – no you ain't, you're the one that said Peter didn't have that so-called fire and he wasn't your type of man. And that Kevin made you feel like a natural woman." "You don't have to rub my nose in it.

I know what I said about the differences between Peter and Kevin. But I've learned my lesson about that so-called fire. Roxanne girl, that so -call fire almost "burned a hole in my heart and cause me to commit murder. I'll take Peter any day, after dealing with a man with that so-called fire. He might not have a six-pack or muscles that jumps out at you, but what Peter does have good looks can't compare. He has the ability to add to my happiness." Said Janice. Roxanne gave her a hug and told her, that she was glad, she was in a happy and healthy relationship. Then Janice asked her to see if she could get some tickets to Mrs. B's' Comedian Show by her mother's house in

Richmond Heights at Theodora's Bar and Grill. Roxanne agreed to try to get the tickets as they both finish lunch and returned back to work. The tickets for the comedy show were sold at several outlets.

Chapter 4

Jackie had gone to stay over at her sister Karen's house for a few days. What Michael had put her through she wanted to be with family. After all, Karen is the only family she has that lives in Pie County. Both of their parents had died in a car accident while traveling from Winter Gardens three years ago. Their father had fallen asleep at the wheel; they never knew what hit them. They died instantly from a head-on collision with an eighteen wheeler.

Karen didn't ask Jackie any questions when she saw her get out the car. It was obvious what had happened to Jackie. Some irresponsible boy in a man's body had lost control of his emotions. My sister was wearing his insecurity around her right eye. Karen thought to herself. She threw her arms around Jackie and was thankful she was alive.

They went into the house and Karen put some African tea on to boil. They sat down on the white leather couch and Jackie began talking. "Well big sis, you always said most men have an identity crisis" Karen responded, "No there are some men, who know who they are as a man and don't have to prove their manhood by abusing a woman physically or verbally. However, you do come across jackasses like our ex-boyfriend's Joe and Michael." Karen went on to tell her about her run-in with her ex-boyfriend Eli. When I first started dating Joe he was a UPS Driver making a good salary. Six months into their relationship, he got into a verbal confrontation with one of the customers. Needless to say, he got fired. Karen went on to tell Jackie about the first and only time Joe put his hands on her. She was trying to tell Eli something for his own good. Eli had lost several jobs by running off at the mouth and she was sick and tired of him leaning on her as a financial crutch. Eli had a bad habit of talking before thinking.

One night they were having a serious discussion after he had gotten fired from another job. "I simply told him sometimes that he says things without considering the consequences afterward. Then I gave him a few examples. How about the time his supervisor asked him to sweep the floor, even though it wasn't part of his job's? description. Since work was kind of slow, he should have gone ahead and swept it. They were still going to pay him 10.50 an hour, no matter what he was doing. Oh no, not him! He had to tell his boss it wasn't part of his job and he wasn't sweeping the floor for no one.

Then a month a later when he was thirty minutes late for work they wrote him up and fired him for being late. It was only his third time being late in a year. The reason they gave him was some lame excuse, that he delayed a large shipment from being shipped out in a timely fashion. Girl, before I could get another word out my mouth the man hauled off and slapped the taste out of my mouth. I had to grab my face to make sure it was still in one piece.

Then I looked at him like he had just lost his god damn mind and asked that dumb ass question. Why did you hit me, Eli? Girl, that man asked me who in the hell did I think I was a damn psychic. How did I know that it was a lame excuse they gave him for why he was fired? He didn't sweep the floor because nobody was going to use him like a flunky? Now that was some dumb shit that came out his mouth. Girl for a few moments, I thought I was listening to a total stranger, this was not the same man I had been dating for the past two years. There was no way he could have changed overnight or maybe I didn't pay attention to the signs.

He apologized and expected great sex after what he had done to me. I screwed him like he had stolen something. I had him moaning like everything was fine. "I love you baby and you're the best thing that ever happened to me and I don't want to lose you," he said with every hump I made. When Eli fell asleep, I went into the kitchen and boiled me some water, the water wasn't hot enough to burn him, just sting him. I got the .38 gun from my car. I creep into the bedroom and that same "slap me hand" was hanging on the side of the bed. I threw that hot water on his hand. You want to see a funny sight, try to imagine a butt-naked man jumping out of the bed, holding his hand and running through the house screaming, with his penis swinging up and down. "Woman did you lose your got damn mind?" he yelled at me. I told him Yeah, I did but that "slap me hand" brought me back to my reality. I told him I was a woman not his personal "slapping bag" and I know love had nothing to do with that slap.

After Eli put some first aid cream on his hand and wrapped his hand with a wet towel, the sucker tried to charge at me. I pulled my .38 gun out of my housecoat and pointed it straight at his face and I told him if he took one more step closer, it would be his last one on earth.

Eli stood stiff as a doorknob and pissed on himself. Girl, my heart was beating so fast, I thought it was going to jump out my chest. I helped Eli packed his shit so fast that night and sent him on his way. I always thought I would be drawing my gun on a stranger instead of the man I loved. I'm so glad I never heard from him again. I don't know why some relationships start out on the right foot and end up on the wrong foot. Love has no enemies. However, some people who once claimed they loved each other become enemies. This type of behavior goes on in all ethnic groups as well as the rich and the poor, usually whenever a man loses control of his emotions. I once read a poem somewhere that didn't make any sense to me then, but now it does. It said "Men are just like an apple, you won't know how sweet or bitter, they are until you take a bite." said Karen. That comment made Karen and Jackie laugh like teenage girls.

Karen's story she shared about Eli, broke the ice for Jackie to start talking about her ordeal with Michael. When I first met Michael, I thought he was a dream come true. I saw him a few times in the Caribbean Café. We both glanced at each other across the room. We must have seen each other about three or four times before he approached me. Here was this tall and fine-as hell man with a million-dollar smile. He could do toothpaste commercials for a living, smelling good enough to sniff all day long, wearing that blue Armani Suit and standing in front of my table asking me what my name was.

Girl, it was so hard for me just to say Jackie from blushing so damn much. He sat down and introduced himself. We talked for almost 45 minutes. He spoke intelligently about the current events going on in the world and he had two jobs. I was so used to dealing with every day run of the mill men who didn't have an intellect beyond the six clock news and sports. Who had the same basic conversation, what's your name, where you work and do you have any children.

He had to go back to work, he asked me for my telephone number. I never believed in a man call me first, so I took his number and waited a few days before calling him. I didn't want to seem desperate. I was so nervous dialing Michael's number there was something different about him. What would I say to Michael on the phone? I didn't want to give Michael the impression that I was an air head. The phone rang two times and I was tempted to hang-up, but a voice on the other end said, "Hello." It was Michael, he answered in a sexy baritone voice. We talked for about fifty minutes or so. He asked me about my dreams and my short-term goals. I found myself getting hot over the phone; girl, the man made me get wet between my legs or I was just horny as hell. I had not had sex for months.

We made plans for dinner that coming Friday at "La Queens" a very expensive restaurant down by the ocean-front. If he was trying to impress me, I was impressed.

He was punctual, 8 o'clock sharp. I had on my "Get it girl" baby blue tight fitting dress with the split up the back. It was slightly low cut in the front and hugging every curve of my hips. Girl, the man couldn't take his eyes off me the whole night. After dinner, I wanted to take Michael back to my apartment and fuck his brains out. I manage to keep a grip on my horny emotions. He gave me a sweet peck on my lips and said good night. I went upstairs smiling so hard, like a young girl with a high school crush.

We went out for about two months or so, before that magical moment happened. We had just come home from an enjoyable evening on the town. Finally, my curiosity was going to be satisfied, "Could he screw, as good as he looked?" I could never have imagined sex being so sensational. Michael was so gentle; we both took off all our clothes. Then we sipped on some red wine and listened to some Barry White on the stereo. Then he started kissing my neck and my back. He took my breast in the palm of his hand and squeezed them tenderly as and if they were ripe tomatoes. Girl, he laid me back on the bed and started licking me everywhere likable. I started climaxing before we ever engaged in actual lovemaking. That kind of pleasure should be against the law. Honey, I couldn't get enough of that man, we must have gone on throughout the entire night. His lovemaking was great and he was a complete gentleman in and out of the bed. The man treated me like I was a queen.

What I wasn't paying attention to, was that Michael was becoming possessive of me. It started out slowly, with manipulating my mind and then my freedom. Every time I would bring up spending time with other people he would say "What about me, don't I count?" I felt guilty about not being with him. He would never give me a direct demand just a request is how he would put it. Like a fool, I fell for that bullshit. I was only feeding his ego while he was gaining control over my mind. I'm glad the "real him" stepped in before I made a big mistake by marrying him.

After their sisterly discussion, they gave each other a hug. Karen and Jackie decided to go to the Springfield Shopping Mall. It was located in the next county that was only forty-five minutes from Karen's house. Buying new things always cheered Jackie up.

They got into Karen's Green Jeep and jumped on the freeway.

Traffic was moving smoothly. Jackie turned on the radio and wouldn't you know, they were playing a song titled "I want to lick you up and down." Jackie flew off the handle and said, "That's what I'm talking about, some men think sex is the solution to a woman's problem. Men start out licking you up and down and then they end up keeping you down, especially if they are thinking with their little head instead of their big head." Karen quickly turned the radio to a jazz station. Karen reassured Jackie, that men in general, are not bad, that just make some fucked up choices, that causes pain in other people's lives.

They finally arrived at the West Gate Shopping Mall. Trying to find a parking space was almost impossible. Eventually, they found one, after driving around in a circle for a few minutes. Just as Karen parked the car and turned off the ignition, Michael popped out of nowhere. He started banging on Jackie's window and yelled, "You no good whore, I told you I was going to get you." He tried to open the car door but it was locked. Jackie was shaking and began crying hysterically. She begging Karen to leave. Karen said, "No, I'm going to put a stop to this shit right now." Karen slid her hand underneath her seat and got her .38 gun. She eased the gun up along the side of her

right leg and opened the car door with her left hand.

She jumped out the car, aimed the gun at Michael and said, "Listen here motherfucker, I don't know what kind of crazy broads you've been dealing with, but my sister isn't one of them. If you ever! I mean ever! Lay another finger on her or even blink your eyes at my sister, when I get through busting a cap in your ass, your own mama won't recognize you. I don't know where in the hell men get off displaying their dysfunctional behavior on women." Michael took a few steps back from Jackie's window. He was shocked.

By then a few spectators had gathered around them. Karen continued talking. "Take a good look at my sister's eye." Michael wouldn't look at Jackie's eye, in fact, he had that same I don't give a damn look all over his face. Karen fired a shot into the ground. "I said look at it got damn it. That's your insecurity she is wearing around her eye. How would you like to be wearing mine in the form of a bullet? If you don't get your sick ass away from my car, my finger might get trigger happy and slip." yelled Karen. Michael ran to his Cadillac, which was illegally parked in the handicap parking space. He drove out of there like a "bat out of hell." "Take me home, I'm no longer in the mood for shopping," said Jackie. She just wanted to get back to Karen's house and relax. They figured out that Michael must have followed them from Karen's house. Since Karen was the only family Jackie had living in Pie County, he knew that was where she would go.

Jackie has always been the total opposite of Karen, like day and night. They both were short and petite, but Karen had an "I don't take no shit attitude". She always stood up for herself and was ready to throw down at any time. On the other hand, Jackie was very passive and easy going. She would have preferred to walk away from a nasty situation instead of solving it, especially if violence was the solution.

Jackie looked over at Karen, while she was driving along the freeway. "Karen where in the world did you get the nerves to stand up to Michael like that? I could never have stood up to Michael with a gun," said Jackie. "Let me tell you something after I was attacked, I went to the gun range and learned how to use a gun. I'm mentally prepared myself to deal with anything that comes my way. Working at the prison also, help take the edge off of fear of men. I would have pulled the trigger and shot him in the leg. Coming after you in broad daylight, just to feed his ego was a stupid move Individuals like Michael, need to seek professional help and women who stay in these type of relationships suffers from L.S.E (low self-esteem). I treat individuals like him every day in my practice.

They finally arrived back home. Jackie needed a stiff drink after that episode with Michael at the shopping mall. She went into the house and poured her and Karen a strong rum and coke drink. They both sat on the couch sipping it slowly. Then Jackie and Karen started reminiscing about their childhood up-brining. Their father had always been a control freak. He controlled their mother through fear of his verbal and sometimes physical abuse. It was hard for them to understand why she stayed with him. Late at night when their parents were fast asleep Karen and Jackie would always discuss their father's dysfunctional behavior he displayed during the day.

Karen recalls one incident in particular that sticks out in her mind. One day their mom stopped by their grandmother's house straight after work because grandma was feeling ill (God bless the dead). Daddy threw a "shit-fit" because dinner wasn't done by the time he arrived home. As soon as their mom walked through the front door, daddy started cussing and yelling at her. He told her if she ever pulled that shit again he would put his foot so far up her butt, they would have to cut his leg off to retrieve it. She tried to explained why she had gotten home late. He told her to shut the fuck up. Their mom rushed into the kitchen and started dinner. The look of sadness and shame was all over her face. She knew Jackie and Karen had overheard every word their father had said to her.

There were a few times Karen came close to giving her daddy a good piece of her mind. However, she thought twice about dipping into grown folk's business. Also, the consequences of talking back to a two-hundred and fifty-pound man and having her teeth knocked out of her mouth was not a good idea. She was too young to be wearing dentures.

Their mother started drinking heavily and their father was clueless. She would pour the soda out the can, then pour Gin and orange juice in it. Watching her mother try to drink her problems away, used to hurt Karen to the core.

Once their mother had contemplated suicide and she was going to make a tape recording of the hell their father had put her through and he was responsible for her taking her own life. It was to be played during her funeral service. She wanted to humiliate and hurt him in the worst possible way. It would have been easier for her just to leave him, however, he had threatened to kill her if she ever tried to leave. She took his threats seriously.

Their mother got help for her drinking problem. As their father got older, he mellowed out a little bit. The only thing Karen regretted was that their mama died never regaining her identity as a woman or fulfilling her dream of owning a catering business.

"Mom took so much shit off of daddy until she could have literally been labeled as a shit-eater. I know that term sounds harsh, however, I use it when I have a client who is in denial of the gravity of the abuse. In order to help her grasp what role she is playing in her relationship. I made a promise to myself, that when I became an adult, I wasn't going to take no shit from a man. Not for his love or financial stability, because I learned from second-hand experience what a man's verbal and physical abuse could do to you," said Karen.

Jackie asked her why she always remembered the negative things about their childhood days. "Girl, I never told you, I had built-resentment towards our father. I traumatized, by our father's abusive behavior, it was hard for me to trust a man with my heart. The first guy I dated in college was abusive towards me, hell after that I thought about becoming a lesbian. I did try it, but that lifestyle wasn't for me, I'm still friends with that young lady today. I don't knock any bodies lifestyle choices as long as they are happy. I had to speak with a therapist about the resentment I had towards our father in order to move on in my life. That why I remember the negative things that happened in our childhood." Jackie was speechless, she gave Karen a hug. "Wow, I had no idea what you went through., I always thought you had your shit together," said Jackie. Karen smiled. "Yes, I got my shit to together now," said Jackie.

They agreed to change the subject to something more pleasant. Jackie said, "Well let's go to church tomorrow. I need to have a serious talk with God." "Yeah, that sounds like a great idea," said Karen. Since Jackie and Karen were almost the same sizes, Jackie could wear one of her Sunday "going-to-meeting" dresses. They watched television until they fell asleep on the sofa. Sometime during the night they woke up and went into the bedrooms and went to sleep.

The next morning, the alarm clock woke Karen up. She went into the guest bedroom and clapped her hands to wake Jackie up. Jackie sat up on the bed and stared at Karen with a blank look on her face. "Get up sleepy head," said Karen. Karen's house had two bathrooms, that made it convenient for them to shower at the same time. Karen showered quickly, in and out was her motto. She put on her blue housecoat and went into the kitchen to make breakfast.

While the grits, eggs, biscuits, and bacon were cooking, Karen turned the radio on. She always enjoyed listening to church music on 909 F.M. radio station. Jackie stayed in the shower a little longer. The warm water felt soothing to her body. Jackie finished showing, dried her body off, then looked in the mirror at her black eye and wonder if the make-up would cover it up. She put on her Karen's red housecoat that hanging behind the door.

She joined Karen in the dining room. They both sat down at Karen's marble dinette table, ate breakfast, sipped on some coffee and small talked before getting dressed for church. The make-up did a pretty good job of covering up Jackie's black eye.

Karen drove them to A.I.M. Baptist Church. They had been going there since they were teenagers. When they reached the entrance of the church the deacons greeted them with a welcome hug. That type of friendliness was one of the things Jackie and Karen liked most about their church beside the pastor's teachings. Pastor Haywood was the new preacher who had taken Reverend Jackson's position when he retired two years ago. Pastor Edward Haywood was in his early forties and good looking too. He stood about 5'8 feet tall, a muscular built with a low Afro. He was soft-spoken but firm at the same time. He was married, but that didn't stop the sisters in the church from fantasizing about him Pastor Haywood messages made you think if you did nothing else.

He studied in Kemet now named Egypt and other parts of Africa for five years after completing seminary school. When he returned to the U.S. he further his learning by taking courses in Black History, America History and Psychology, at the local college. He was inspired to become a preacher, through the stories his grandma shared during his visits with her. The first stories she shared was after young Edward and his grandmother returned from church. His grandmother asked him how did he like the service. Edward replied, the singing was good, but the pastor's message sounded just like your pastor's message grandmother.

His grandmother smiles and told him to come sit next to her on the sofa. Edward sat down on the sofa, his grandmother took his small hand and put her hand on top. "Son, when I was a little girl, my grandmother explained to me how religion is one of the most powerful the sky". They were so far removed from their own African spirituality, it was easier to just adapt to the Europe religion, generation after generation. Some Black folks feel by going to church they are pleasing God, even though no one knows for sure."

His grandma chuckled after explaining the ideology of the black church. Edward looked at his grandmother strangely and said "that doesn't make any sense grandma. Why don't black people think for themselves? How do they know if everything the preacher is telling them is the truth?" "Child, I don't know and I'm too old to be questioning religion now. I just go along with the program, hoping I get my pie in the sky." She chuckled again.

"Well grandmother when I get older I'm going to become a preacher and I'm going to search for the truth and preach the truth". His grandmother gave him a big hug and said you do just that.

It wasn't easy for some of the congregation to adapt to his method of teaching. Reverend Haywood, was not your traditional black preacher who just stirred up the congregation spirits, he stimulated their minds as well. He knew God was too big and powerful to have been confined to just one book.

It wasn't easy for Pastor Haywood to change traditional black preaching. Oh no, those Elders in the church were ready to put up a fight against "change". The fight began after the Pastor Haywood's second church service which coincided with the monthly church meeting. The mothers and elders of the church noticed that during his first two services he never asked anyone to come up and give their lives to God, which was a problem with the elders of the church.

During the monthly church meeting, it was the first topic of discussion. Jackie was the church secretary and was present during the meeting to take notes. One of the younger members named Randy had already forewarned Pastor Haywood about this issue, therefore he was prepared. Mother Baskins who had been attending the church for over 30 years led the meeting by asking "How dare you to come into God's house and make that type of change. There are a lot of lost souls out there in the world, that need to give their lives to God." Rev. listened tentatively to Mother Baskins and few others tell him how it has always been done.

He asked them three questions. First of all, how do you know for a fact that when they come down to the altar to give their lives to God, that is what takes place? Secondly, how can you give God something that already belongs to the Creator (God)? Has anyone died, gone to heaven and came back and told you that is what happens when they come to the altar call? Thirdly, when did you take your life from God? That's some deep programming, for us to have the audacity to think we have the power to take something from God and when we are ready, we can give it back to God.

Let me ask you a question, do the Rabbi as their members to give their lives to God or the Catholics Priest? Silence filled the air and if looks could kill, Rev. would have been 6 feet under. Mother Baskin folded her arms and rolled her eyes and looked away from Rev. read a scripture from the book of Hosea 4 "My people are destroyed for lack of knowledge." He went all to say, most of you are physically alive around like zombies. You are scared to think for yourselves and Lord have mercy on you if you think outside the "traditional Christian church box." One of the most powerful things God gave you was your mind. That is the only part of the human body man can't see or touch physically. You need to know more than biblical scriptures. Even Dr. King knew he had to use more than scriptures for change to come about, he took action.

Randy was eager with curiosity, he broke the ice, well Rev. you've pissed the elders of the church off. However, I'm eager to learn something different. Rev. smile and said that is exactly what I intend to do. Take a good look at the members of our church most of them are struggling from paycheck to paycheck. I'm sure the same struggling spirit goes on in other churches as well. Members come to church, get high off the message and their spirit dance to songs from the choir. When Monday rolls around they are facing the same crap they were facing from the previous week. In order for them to change their lives, they have to change lives. I know that sounds strange but it's true. If you attend a church and the Pastor don't give you information that makes you think, then he or she has not done their job. God doesn't want zombies, he wants conquers who can positively impact their own lives and the lives of everyday people.

He had the members to research where the words to the age-old song Amazing Grace originated from. The church members were shocked to find out the words written by an individual who was a slave trader named John Newton who went to Africa and kidnapped Africans. His slave ship was about to sink when he pleaded to God for help and the ship didn't sink. The lyrics to Amazing Grace came to him. Pastor Haywood also had them research the definition of the word "wretch" which is in the song Amazing Gracing. The definition reads as follows: a miserable person, unhappy person, despicable or vile person. The description of a wretch described Newton, not you said, Pastor Haywood. He challenged everyone in this meeting to go without watching television for a week and will meet after church.

Now if that didn't put the icing on the cake I don't know what did. Some of the members mumbled under their breath who does he think he is God? All twenty of the members in the meeting took on the challenge of not watching television for a week.

Their attitudes were different during the next meeting. They gave testimonies of how they were able to accomplish tasks, that they had put off. Television is not there to educate you, their purpose is to entertain and program you, said Pastor Haywood. Everyone had something positive to say even Mother Baskin. She smiled and said that she had prayed about this new way of preaching. She took a hard look at her community and realized something new was needed in the church. She also said they were repeating history without realizing it. The elders stop teaching the youth. The Elders are coming to church, sitting on the pulpit and are waiting to die, so they could get their pie in the sky. Everyone burst out into laughter. Mother Baskin also shared a conversation she had wither nephew Tariq during the week of no television. Tariq told her that if Dick Gregory at the age of 84 years old was still out there giving information to help change the black community until his death, what was wrong with the elders in the black churches? The only thing the elders could do was pray and take no action. Mother Baskin said, her eyes got big and her mouth fell open. He didn't say it to be disrespectful, but this was his image of the elders in the church. That statement made her take a good look at herself and the elders in the church and she knew then that Pastor Haywood method of preaching was needed. The members said Amen and Rev. Haywood gave Mother Baskin a big hug.

After a year of preaching and teaching, the church members who were receiving public assistance in the form of food stamps became entrepreneurs and investors. He used the story of Curtis "wall street" Carroll to teach them. Curtis went to prison when he was 17 years old, for robbery and 1st degree-murder. He was given 54 years to life. He grew-up during the crack era, his mother and grandmother both were crack addicts. He couldn't read or write when he entered prison. He would have someone read the sports section of the newspaper to him. Because he couldn't read, Curtis picked of the stock-market section of the paper by mistake. When he handed the other inmate the paper to read to him, he was told it was the stock market section. He asked the inmate what was the stock-market. He told him it was where rich white people made their money. That statement turned on a light in Curtis mind, it led him to learn how to read and write. He learned how to read the stock-market, he gave correctional guards tips on their retirement. He has his family invest in the stocks he picked. He became so good at the stock-market, that the warden made him teach the other inmates how to read and invest in the stock-market. Curtiss was interviewed by magazines and television personnel. When he gets out of prison, he will be richer and wiser than when he went in. Curtiss story was the fuel that was needed to motivate the church members who received food stamps to utilize the minds to the fullest.

Karen and Jackie found a seat in the crowded church on the back row. Pastor Haywood asked his congregation the question, "Who Are You"? The church members yelled out "Great People Who God Created", Pastor Haywood shook his head in agreement and said amen. At the beginning of each month, Pastor Haywood not only brought in books about the journey of black people and other books to help expand the minds of the members. One that caught the eyes of the members was "Think and Grow Rich" written by Napoleon Hill. Pastor Haywood had started a book fund at the church to continue purchasing books. Every Sunday, he would go over part of the book of the month and continue discussing the book during bible study.

You cannot contain God in a box or one book. God is in everything and everybody. Pastor Haywood knew all the members were experiencing different things in their lives, therefore he had developed a class on Thursday night, to help the members learn how to utilize their minds to change the course of the lives. One of the books he used to teach was by Dr. Joseph Murphy titled "The Power of Your Subconscious mind." He knew most of the congregation were only using 10%, just like most people outside the church.

He was determined that he would change the tradition of the church that had plagued the black community. Preachers who had inherited a slavery mentality. A preacher has a responsibility to God, himself and the members of his church to go beyond tradition. God did not die in the book of revelation? He is still alive today. He told the church members to stop looking for God on the outside, He resides

within you. He created you in His own image. He would share quotes such as "repetition is the mother of learning, the father of action and the architect of accomplishment". Tap into your greatness and stop

blaming the devil for your bad choices and accept the consequences that come from them. That is the only way people who claim to know God will grow.

Wherever you are in life, as an adult it is because of the decisions you made. Whatever bad choices you make in life, the collateral damage will be your children. Another thing, that age-old lie "God is testing you" that lie was told to black church people when unwanted situations showed up in their lives. No other ethnic group was told that "lie" except black folks. That lie keeps you from doing a self-evaluation to make positive changes within yourself. Pastor Haywood was particular about what type of spiritual songs would be sung. He realized a lot of the church songs, were sorrowful and even the ones with a high temple always talked about a struggle, like "I'm climbing up on the rough side of the mountain trying to make it in". What does Proverb 18:21 say "the tongue has the power of life and death."

Karen and Jackie enjoyed Pastor Haywood's new method of teaching, it had helped them find balance in their lives. No matter what crap showed up in their lives, they knew the God in them could handle it. The choir sang "It's The God In Me" by Mary-Mary. Pastor Haywood, always closed by telling the members to go out into the world and leave their mark of greatness.

Jackie and Karen went to Chantel's Cafeteria after church to have an early dinner. They both laughed and talked about the church service throughout their meal. By the time they arrived back home from Chantel's Cafeteria, Jackie had made up her mind to take her vacation earlier than originally planned.

She decided to travel to Africa. She always wanted to see the Pyramids. She felt as though she had come too close to death, at the hands of Michael not to enjoy life. Too many people die without going to happen to her. Also, the change of scenery would do her mind and body a lot of good.

However, she was too scared to go over to her apartment. She phoned Janice and asked her to go over there and pick up a few of her belongings and bring them to her. Janice agreed. Karen and Jackie watched a good movie on television, relaxed and fell asleep. Janice was a little spooked about going over there alone, so she asked Peter to ride along. Jackie had phoned ahead to notify the apartment manager that they were coming.

They arrived at Jackie's house and the building manager let them into Jackie's apartment. Janice quickly gathered Jackie's belongings and put them in a suitcase. As they were getting ready to leave, Janice noticed the red light on Jackie's answering machine blinking. Janice decided to listen to Jackie's messages and tell her about them. The first message was her doctor's office reminding her of an appointment and then Michael's threating message. Peter and Janice looked at each other with disbelief. "He must me be crazy, how could you want to harm someone you love," said Peter. "Should I tell Janice about the message?" Janice asked "No, Janice has been through enough." said Peter. They took Jackie's belongings to her and never mentioned the message Michael left on her answering machine.

Jackie phoned West Point Airport to check the time for the earliest flight to Africa. The reservation clerk told her 9 p.m. that night and the next flight was in two days. Jackie had to get her vaccination shots. She made reservations for the flight leaving in two days. Jackie was an interior decorator at Art Deco Designers. Her boss Frank was one of the nicest men you would ever want to work for. He gave Jackie her first break after she finished Florida A.M. University. Jackie phoned Frank and informed him she was having some personal problems and needed to take her vacation now. Frank agreed and wanted to know if there was anything he could do to help her. Jackie said she had everything under control.

Jackie packed her bags and borrowed some of Karen's cloths.

Karen had phoned a friend who was a doctor to assist Jackie with giving her the vaccination shots. Two days. later Karen took her to the airport and she was on her way to. Africa.

Chapter 5

The next morning the alarm clock buzzed loudly at 5:30. a.m. The sound of the wind-driven raindrops pelting against the window pane startled Karen for a moment as she dragged herself out of bed. A good hot shower was definitely what she needed to arouse her body. She strolled into the bathroom and turned the shower on. She waited a few minutes until the hot steam built up before removing her pink nightgown and stepped into the shower. The bathroom was quickly filled with steam from the running water. She positioned her limp body, head first, directly underneath the running water, while swaying her head back and forth slowly. She lathered her entire body with some "shock it to me" soap. Her body felt revived after the shower.

She dried her body off and blow dried her hair, only to pull it back into a ponytail. She stared in the mirror for a few seconds admiring her beauty, something she had much to be thankful for.

Four years ago, while she was stopped at a red light, a rock came flying through her windshield and robber reached into her car to snatch her purse which was laying on the seat. Karen resisted by grilling her teeth into the mugger's arm, which wasn't a smart thing to do. The robber punched her in the face a couple of times, pulled out a switchblade and sliced her face up like a butcher. On top of that, the robber took her purse and got away, leaving her with a broken jawbone, nose, and a sliced up face. The doctors at Mount Sinai Hospital did remarkable plastic surgery on her face. They had to remove some skin tissue from her buttocks to use on the cuts on her face.

Karen went into her bedroom, slid on her faded blue jeans and a red T-shirt, along with her white sneakers. This type of casual wear was appropriate for her visits to the U-Horn Prison. It always puts the inmates in a relaxed mood when talking to her.

It was dark outside due to the daylight saving time. Karen went into the kitchen and fixed herself a ham sandwich and grabbed a soda out the refrigerator. Just as she reached for a brown bag out of the pantry, all the lights went out in the house. Her heart started pumping rapidly and she was scared out of her wits. She kneeled down by the window, pulled the curtains slightly back and peeped out. She didn't see anyone. The howling sound of the wind blowing against the tree limbs was the noise she heard and the street lights shined in her yard. Then the horrible thoughts, of Michael coming back for revenge raced through her mind. Just as she sat down on the couch, the sound of glass breaking at the back door sent Karen into a panic. She hopped up and made her way to the china cabinet where her emergency flashlight was hanging on the side. She grabbed it off the hook and switched it on, to search for the phone. She spotted the phone on the floor next to the couch, she got down on the floor and crawled over to it.

She began dialing "911". Before she could dial the last "1", a bright light shined brightly in her face, blinding her, from the doorway leading to the kitchen. All she could see was a shadow of a tall individual, who in a stern voice, ordered her to put that damn phone down. Karen dropped the phone and her flashlight. She had only heard Michael's voice once and she wasn't sure if it was him. "What do you want?" Karen yelled out. There was silence for a minute, then the person told her to lay on the floor face down. Karen did as she was told. The person told her to close her god damn eyes and count from 100 to 1.

Just as she started counting out loud, she heard footsteps on the broken glass, she didn't know if they were coming towards her or walking away. She started praying, that the God that was in this individual, wouldn't let him kill her. She didn't hear anymore footsteps, she slowly opened her eyes and got her flashlight. She shined it at the door and no one was there. She phoned the police. She went outside and turned her circuit breaker back on. The police arrived and she made a report. Karen couldn't tell them who the person was that broke into her house. She did tell them about the incident that happened between her and Michael at the shopping mall. The police told her that they would speak to Michael. She didn't know Michael's phone number or address. She would have to get that information from her sister when she returned from her trip.

Karen wasn't going to let the incident stop her from doing her job, at U-Horn Prison. It was 6:45 now, Karen phoned her handyman David and asked him to come over and fix her back door window. She also requested him to install a security alarm system as soon as possible. She hung up the phone, went into the kitchen and finish packing her lunch. By now that hot shower had worn off and she felt as though she had run around the block a few times. She switched the answering machine on, just in case Jackie called. Then she grabbed her briefcase from the hallway closet and checked inside for her miniature tape recorder along with her evaluation data sheets. Everything she needed was in place. She picked up her keys off the coffee table and headed out the door. Once she got into her car, she pulled out the driveway in a hurry.

She entered onto highway 27 it was a shortcut to the U-Horn Prison. Also, the scenery of Harrison National Forrest along this route was a beautiful sight. Most of the pine trees had reached their full height in time for the Christmas harvest and watching the raccoons and dears dotting along the outskirts of the forest was always exciting to see.

Karen wanted to arrive at U-Horn at least twenty minutes before interviewing the first inmate. Those extra minutes allowed her time to review the files in order to know a little bit about the inmates before interviewing them.

She finally reached the U-Horn Prison. As she drove into the parking lot, she checked her watch to see how much time she still had on her side. It was 7:35 a.m., it was enough time for her to review a few inmate files. Her first session started at 8:00 o'clock on the dot. Everything in the prison ran according to schedule.

She grabbed her briefcase and lunch, and hurried out the car. As she quickly strolled towards the entrance of the prison, she passed Correctional Officer Whitehead, who greeted her with a big friendly smile and hello as she walked by. Whitehead had tried to go out on a thought he was full of himself and there wasn't enough of him left over for her to compete with.

She walked over to the window titled "Personnel Entrance", to obtain her visitor's pass. Then she took the elevator to the fifth floor where the "prayer room" was located. This room was assigned to Karen by the warden. It used to be an extra break room for the correctional officers, now the inmates use it for church service. It was a cozy, isolated room located in the far left-wing corner away from any distractions.

Karen quickly entered the prayer room and sat down in the big black chair. She placed her briefcase on top of the desk and shoved her lunch into one of the empty drawers. Then she picked up the five files sitting on the desk. She always spent half of her day there, which allowed her to see at least five inmates each time she visited. They were usually chosen at random by the warden or upon her request to see one of the inmates she had previously seen. Seldom did any of the inmates make a request to see her on their own.

Karen glanced at the names on the files and she quickly noticed one of them didn't have a batch of printouts showing a list of prior criminal cases. She put the other four files down on the desk and quickly browsed through this one. The name on the outside of the file read "James Washington". This usually was a good sign, meaning that the inmate could probably be a good candidate for being rehabilitated, as long as he wasn't serving a life sentence. Karen reads the inmate's history sheet which indicated that this young man who finished high school and attended three years of college at a major university. He was now serving a 5-year sentence for armed robbery, but due to overcrowding, in the prison, he would be eligible for parole in a few weeks, even though he had only been in prison for three and a half years.

How could someone have gotten off track like this, Karen thought to herself. She put the file down and picked up the phone and called the warden to cancel seeing two of the five inmates. She was a little drained from the scary ordeal at her house and wanted to finish early. The warden didn't question her decision, after all, she was a damn good psychiatrist.

No sooner had Karen hung up the phone, the guard was bringing in the first inmate. Here was this tall, medium built looking man by the name of Danny Stoneberger. His face was as smooth a baby's butt, his eyes were cold and he was buff from lifting weights.

Karen stood up and greeted him with a gentle hello. His hands and feet were shackled this was the procedure used on inmates convicted of murder. Normally they were escorted in without the cuffs and the guard remained on the outside of the door. There was a panic button at Karen's disposal on the inside of the desk if things ever got out of hand. Have a seat, Karen said. Then she introduced herself as Dr. Karen McDaniel, however, he could call her Karen if that made him feel comfortable. "Is there anything you would like to discuss today Danny?" Karen asked. He stared at her for a few moments before saying a word. Karen was used to this type of reaction from the inmates. They often contemplated if they should really trust her with their dark secrets about their lives. Once they decided that she could be confided in, they usually opened up and began talking. Danny was no different, he eventually started talking about how he killed his wife Gloria. "What happened?" she asked.

I was in love with her, we were high school sweethearts. Gloria was the first woman, I had sex with. Two years after we finished high school, we got married and had two kids together. I went "to work every day and brought all my money home to her. She was a great mom to our daughters, I helped out with the kids whenever she wanted to go out somewhere. I didn't run around in the streets looking for extra material sex. In Gloria, I had more than enough to keep me happy as a man. I thought she felt the same way about me, I guess I was wrong. I never once raised my hand to hit her. I saw enough of that done to my mother and I know she didn't like it. We did argue, but who doesn't.

For about two months, I noticed every Tuesday Gloria started going over to her mother's house at the same time. At first, it didn't bother me, but whenever I would ask her to stay home on a Tuesday she would get upset and threaten to leave me. I didn't want that. Eventually, that Tuesday shit started bothering, I knew something was going on and it wasn't at her mother's house. In my mind I prayed, she was cheating on me but in my heart, I felt she was.

I followed her on Tuesday, and sure enough, my worst fears came true. She was meeting another man a block away from her mother's house. I watched her get into his White Mustang Convertible and they drove to a sleazy motel. They were in the room for about five minutes before I walked over and peeped in the window. In my mind, I was hoping they weren't screwing, but in my gut, I knew they were. I watched him holding her legs up and stroking the hell out of her. She laid there enjoying every bit of it. It hurt me so bad I didn't know what to do.

I went back to my car and sat there for a few minutes contemplating what to do next. The little voice in my head said to drive away but something inside of me wouldn't let me leave. I pounded the steering wheel with my fist over and over again. Then I snapped, I got the bat that I kept in my trunk, went to the front door and kicked it in. The look of fear on her face when she saw me standing in the doorway, hunts me right to this day. She tried to cover her naked body, and he asked who the hell was I. I stared him in the face and said, I'm her motherfucking husband. Who the hell are you? He grabbed his pants and jumped out the window before I could bust his head open with the bat.

She tried to apologize but I head a deaf ear to whatever bullshit she was going to tell me. I walked towards her with the bat in my hand, she started yelling. I dropped the bat and grabbed her by the throat and chocked all the life out her body. By the time I realized what I had done, I cuddled her lifeless body in my arms. Tears ran down my face. I couldn't believe what I had done. The police rushed into the room with their guns drawn, ordered me to stand up and put my hands behind my back. I did. They checked Gloria's arm for any vital signs, there were none. She was gone. I guess the dude who jumped out the window must have called them. They pulled the sheet over her body and escorted me out to the police car. I was I was arrested and placed in the police car. The ambulance arrived, retrieved Gloria's lifeless body and took it to the morgue.

At my Pre-trial court appearance, I pleaded guilty to second-degree-murder. It was a crime of passion. Now all I think about are my two girls growing without their parents. Killing their mother was a selfish act on my part. All I thought about was my pain, not the pain I would cause our children, her family, and mines. Sure they have a grandma and aunties, but nothing could replace the love of a mother or father. I should have walked away and never looked back, but my ego wouldn't let me.

It has been four years since I last saw my kids and I miss them so much. They are staying with Gloria's mother and she refuses to bring them to see me. I know the last thing they remember about me was being handcuffed placed in the backseat of a police car and their mother being taken away with a sheet covered over her entire body. I can't change that, but I love them and I can't change that either. I have been working in the laundry room saving every dime I earn to send to them. Karen, if you could do me one big favor, and I have no right to ask this of you. I have already spoken to the warden about sending my money to them. He got it approved through the proper channels. If you could take it to them and let them know how much I love them and they will always be in my heart. I would appreciate it very much.

My two girls are ten and six years old now. I know they don't understand why I killed their mom and I don't expect them to forgive me. I just want them to know that I will always love them. That would be enough for me.

Karen was shocked by what she had just heard. Here was a man behind bars trying to support his kids. Karen's heart went out to this man. She couldn't justify what he had done, talking someone's life is committing the unthinkable act. However, she felt sad that love had to end in death. She gave him a book on "Acts of Faith" by Ms. I. Vanzant as well a book title "Vision For Black Men" by Mr. N.

Akibar. These books had been previously approved by the warden, for her to give to the prisoners. She spoke with him for a while about his upbringing. She pointed out the trigger moments during his childhood that could have contributed to why he made the awful choice to kill his wife. Too often, children grow up without love and as adults, they based love on how they feel. It becomes hard for them to define what love is and what love is not. There are a lot of books out there to help people become better individuals. Sadly, most people who need self-improvement don't think anything is wrong with them. Therefore, these individuals repeat the pattern of raising children without knowing the meaning of love.

She told Danny about a male client of hers, who expressed his love for his two sons, by buying them the latest tennis shoes and clothes wear. He didn't know spending quality time with them was more valuable than material items. He refused to give the mother of his two sons financial help with the household bills even though his two sons benefitted from them. Sadly, this client was a prisoner of his upbringing. He was stubborn. He wasn't interested in hearing anything Karen had to say about his parenting skills or lack of them. He walked out her office and never returned.

Tears begin running down Danny's face, he put his hands over his face to wipe the tears, after listening to Karen's story about her clients. He knew he would never be able to replace the precious time he has lost, with his daughters. She gave him some tissue. She told him he can't change the past and being in prison was the consequences of his actions. He understood. He dried his eyes. She agreed to take the money to his daughters and tell them exactly what he said. She asked Danny if he wanted to meet with her again the next time she came. He agreed to see her again. Then Karen pushed the button for the guard to come and escort Danny back to his cell. Danny left out the room with a big smile of relief.

Karen picked up the next file, another murdered. This young man was involved in a gang called the "12 Avenue thugs". He was convicted of killing a 7-year-old girl, during a drive-by shooting. It took five minutes before the guard returned with this inmate whose name was Fred Walker. He was also shackled by the hands and feet.

She greeted him in the same friendly manner she did Danny. But his response wasn't friendly. Fred nodded his head. After Fred sat down, Karen asked him if there was anything he wanted to discuss. Nineteen-year-old Fred, responded, "Bitch can you get me out of here?

That's all I want to discuss. If you can't help do that, then don't waste my damn time trying to read my mind. Cause it ain't going to happen now or never. I'm not a god damn freak or anything. Do you hear me home-girl!" Karen was mad as hell at his response. She responded anyway, "Look here jackass, I didn't put you in here? Did I? I don't look like your lawyer, and I'm damn show don't look like your mother, so don't be calling me no bitch. Now if you don't want to talk that is fine with me." She pressed the panic button and the guard rushed into the office. "You can take him back where you got him from." The guard quickly removed Fred from the room. Karen was a little rattled by the time James Washington was brought to the room.

He came in with a gentle smile on his face, without the handcuffs. Thank God, Karen needed someone with a different demeanor, after speaking with Fred. She greeted him with a smile and a handshake as she introduced herself and told him a seat. Here was this ordinary tall, slender man sitting in front of her. He had a gentle smile on his face. She asked how was he doing, a different introductory from the previous two. Fine and yourself, he responded. Fine, she said.

Karen immediately started asking James questions. Very

directly, she asked, "Can you please tell me how you went from attending college to being behind bars for strong-arm robbery?" "James was taken back for a moment, because he didn't expect Karen to ask that question first. He paused for a few minute and responded, "I can't blame anybody but myself. I had my dreams in the palm of my hand and I lost it. Once I went away to college, my mindset hanged. During my third year at Macca University. Man, people were throwing money at me left and right and "girls" were knocking at my door like room service. I thought I was bigger than life. I became popular during basketball season. Once we won the NCAA championship and I scored the winning basket. I was voted most valuable player and the news media had already mentioned that I'd make the Pros probably by my fourth year. I was moving faster than my feet. I felt as though I had everything under control.

First, it started with my grade average dropping, and then I started slacking off in practice. I felt as though they needed me, I didn't need them. Before I realized what was happening during my third year, I was sitting face to face with the dean, who told me I was being dropped from the basketball team because of academics. There went my scholarship down the drain. The next year I pretended like I was still going to college. I told my mom I had a basketball injury, therefore, I wouldn't be playing. I was rooming with my friends' in their apartments off campus. Whenever she would phone me at the dorm, one of my home-boys would take a message for me. I would call her back as if nothing was wrong. I pulled this deception off for a year and a half.

Then it all came to end during my fourth year. It was during the Christmas holiday when I went home because I needed some money. I had planned to rob some unlikely victim while they were withdrawing money from an ATM machine. Wrong move! What I didn't know was there had been a couple of robberies at this particular ATM machine and the police were on staked out there. I got a gun from one of my friends, it had no bullets in it. I waited until I saw my prey and went to rob him. Before I knew what was happening, I was being handcuffed and put in the back of the police car.

Bam, here I am! The greatest disappointment was lying to my mom. She is the one person I felt bad about letting down. She had worked hard her whole life in hopes of seeing her children finish college. Secondly for making a stupid decision to commit robbery. To top that off, I thought my mother wouldn't find out about my arrest. As fate would have it, one of my home-boys from the neighborhood saw me getting arrested. I know he meant well by going to my house and informing my mother. I would have done anything for her not to find out. The look on her face when she came to see me in the jail, told a thousand stories of a mother's pain. Tears ran down her face as she stared at me through the glass. Then tears begin running down my face, as I looked at the hurt in my mother's face. She placed her hand on the glass and said, son, I love you.

As we both dried the tears from our eyes, she reminded me of her favorite quote that she told me and my siblings. "You only have one moment to make the right choice, so choose wisely. No matter what choices you make, I will always love you. Son, you could have told me about the situation in college. I know college is not for everyone". Those words hit me like a ton of bricks. Then she smiled and said it will be alright and at that moment I wished I could have felt the warmth of my mother's arms around me.

Bam, here I am! The greatest disappointment was lying to my mom. She is the one person I felt bad about letting down. She had worked hard her whole life in hopes of seeing her children finish college. Secondly for making a stupid decision to commit robbery. To top that off, I thought my mother wouldn't find out about my

She was a single parent, but my father kept in touch with us. He provided financially, for me and my sister Brittney's well-being. When I was a shorty he was the one who took me to the basket court and taught me how to play basketball. When I was in the eleven grade, his job relocated out of state and he moved with his job. He kept in touch by telephone and letters.

When I first arrived in prison, I made a collect call to my father and told him what happened. Although he was disappointed in the stupid decision I had made, he still gave me words of encouragement. He said, "Son you screwed up your plan "A" now what is your plan "B", failure is not an option." I told him I would come up with a plan "B" while in prison. I have nothing but time on my hand. He told me he loved me and still believed in me. My father always believed that if your plan "A" didn't work out, you must create a plan" B". Karen asked him what was his plan "B"? He chuckled and told her he had not finalized it yet. "Let me know when you do.", said Karen. "No problem. I have been in here for three and half years and hopefully will be getting out of here in a few weeks due to the overcrowding in prison" said James.

While listening to James, Karen couldn't explain this sexual desire she was feeling just from listening to his soothing voice. She had never been aroused like this before. Her panties became wet and she had to excuse herself to go to the bathroom before she lost all self-control and attacked this man sexually. "Excuse me James, I have to step out to the ladies' room." She got up quickly and exited the room. The bathroom was located outside the room. The guard went inside the room with James until Karen returned. Once she entered the bathroom she went to the sink, turned on the faucet to throw some cold water on her face. Her heartbeat was thumping fast and her body was lusting for a man who was a convicted criminal. Could this sexual attraction be happening because she hasn't had any sex for months? She wiped her face clear of the water and stared in the mirror, only to see a horny psychiatrist. Her nipples were standing at attention. hard as a rock. She gasped for fresh air and left out the ladies' room, walking slowly. She could feel her vagina twitching out of control. Before entering the room, she looked at her watch, it was 11:30 a.m. She went back into the praying room and James stood up to greet her like a gentleman.

While she was out of the room, James had thoughts of her floating around in his mind. Those blue jeans she was wearing showed all of her nice curves. Reality also popped into his mind as well, how could someone of her stature, be interested in someone like him. It had been a long time since he met a woman, who wasn't a "thot" and wasn't only talking to him because he was, "a basketball star".

As she walked closer to her desk, James' manhood began squirming in his pants. When she was one step away from him, he jumped in her path to meet her face to face and embraced her with a warm sensational kiss. Karen didn't resist at first but soon pulled herself away from him after a second or two. "James have you lost your damn mind or something," she said in a firm voice. He quickly apologized, "I'm so sorry Karen I don't know what came over me, but it will never happen again." Karen replied, "I don't know what kind of woman you think I am, but I'm not the easy lay and what makes you think I would get involved with a convict she said with a half-smile on her face?" Then she told him their session was over today. "Can I see you again on your next visit?" he asked. Sure, it's part of my job to assist you, she said in a girlish way. He then stood up and shook her hand and said, it's been a pleasure talking with you.

Karen pushed the button for the guards to come in and take James back to his cell. Once James had been removed from the room, she leaned back against the door exhaling, behind the cheap thrill she had just encountered. She walked over to the jail phone and called Warden Jones, to request the paperwork for Danny's check to be released to her.

Warden Jones informed her it would take about twenty-five minutes to have all the paperwork completed and notarized. She hung up the phone and began filling out her evaluation sheets and made a notation at the bottom, to see Danny and James again on her next visit. Once she completed the evaluation sheets, she sat back and started fantasizing about James in a sexual manner. He's been locked up for a few years and she haven't had any for, she bet he can make her see stars. She snapped back to reality at the sound of the phone ringing. It was the warden, calling back to let her know the paperwork was ready. She told him she would be right down to pick them up. The warden's office was located on the fourth floor of the prison. She quickly grabbed her lunch out of the drawer and picked up her briefcase and headed to the elevator. The elevator took a few minutes before arriving.

When Karen reached the fourth floor, one of the guards was waiting to escort her to the warden's office. Warden Jones was a distinguishable looking man with salt and pepper hair. "Come right in

Karen and have a seat," he said. Karen sat down and looked over the paperwork to make sure Danny's signature had been notarized. "Do I sign here on this line Karen asked?" "Yes, you do, my dear and I will sign as a witness," he said. Karen and Warden Jones signed the three forms, then he turned the check over to Karen. Before leaving his office, Karen requested to see Danny and James on her next visit. Warden Jones wrote down her request. They small talked for a few minutes, then Karen walked over to the elevator, it came faster this time.

No sooner had the elevator doors closed and moved between the fourth and third floor, when the riot alarm sounded. Correctional Guards Sgt. Ayeska and Bernie Tabares, were on duty in the main camera station, which gave her access to all the cameras in the prison. Once she saw the prisoners taking over the 3rd floor, she pushed the riot alarm button. The riot alarm automatically shuts the power off to all the elevators. Karen started screaming, "help! I'm stuck in the elevator."

The guard who was stationed by the elevator ran quickly to get the warden. should follow procedures or not. The prison's guidelines didn't permit him to use it once the riot alarm went off. There are three elevators in total and there was no way to know if the other two had any crazy inmates were on them. Then he thought about his wife and children waiting back home for him. He turned around and headed back into his office. That was a tough decision for the warden to make.

Just as the warden was sitting his black leather chair, the phone rang, it was one of the guards on the third floor. In a hushed voice, he informed the Warden of the situation of the third and second floors. The guards who were stationed in the camera booth on the second and third floor were the first to be taken as hostages along with the other

guards. The inmates determined what time the take-over would take place on each floor. The inmates had staged a fight in front of both camera stations. It appeared that one inmate was being jumped by five other inmates. Without thinking the guards came out the booth to assist the other guards who were trying to break up the fights. The inmates had created their own form of tear gas mixture some flour and black pepper that had been stolen from the kitchen. The homemade mixture of tear gas was thrown into the guard's eyes and blinded them for a few seconds. The prisoners had taken all the guards on both floors hostage and they were trying to get to the fourth floor.

Before the guard could mutter another word out of his mouth, one of the prisoners snatched the phone out of his hand. "Hello who is this?" the prisoner asked. "Who is this?" the warden asked. This T-bone from cell-block "D" and we have some demands we like to have met." "This is not the right way to go about making a request, innocent people can be hurt or killed." "This sounds like the warden, how does it feel motherfucker, not to be in control? I'm tired of the way you run shit around here. I'm running shit now. I'm not making a request, god damn it, I'm telling you what we want. I'm calling all the shots now," T-bone said. "T-bone if anybody gets hurt, I'm holding you personally responsible, do you hear me." "So what, you're going to give me another life sentence, big shit, I wasn't going to see the outside of these prison gates anyway."

T-Bone had his own philosophy if you want to get a man's attention you kill his dog, if you want to send him a message you kill his mother. That why he was doing life in prison. He was already doing a twenty-year scratch for murder and he wanted the witness who testified against him killed. Unfortunately, for T-Bone after the witness was found with their tongue cut out and shot in the head, they retrieved the prison phone records and was able to decode the hit, he had made on the witness. He was sentenced to life. "Click" T-Bone, T-Bone" the warden cried out with only a dial tone responding.

The warden quickly called Governor Sherley Auguste to inform her of the prison takeover. He could not give an exact status of the riot conditions on the second and third floors. Governor Auguste told Warden Jones she was going to order the National Guard to be on standby if the situation wasn't under control in the next 4 hours. Warden Jones also informed the governor of the situation with Karen being stuck in the elevator. The governor ordered the warden to follow normal protocol because more lives would be at stake if the prisoners got to the first floor. The warden hung up the phone not knowing what to do, the security cameras had been destroyed on the second and third floors by the prisoners. He sat still, waiting for further instructions from T-bone or the governor.

Meanwhile, Karen was exhausted because the air conditioner had been turned off and the big old fan was circulating hot air. With what little strength she had left, Karen knocked on the elevator doors, one last time. It just so happened that James was one of the prisoners assigned to watch the movement of the elevators. Karen mustered up enough strength to holler out, "Help me please help me!" James quickly put his ear to the door, just in time to hear Karen's desperate cry for help. He knew it was a woman's voice and wondered if it could be Karen inside.

He looked down the hallway, the coast was clear, then he knocked on the elevator and yelled Karen is that you in there? "Yes it's me," she responded in a weak voice. "Please get me out of here." He told her to stay calm and don't make any more noise, there's no telling how T-Bone may react, having her as a hostage. It could turn deadly, James said. Just as he finished talking to Karen, someone tapped him on the shoulder. James turned around and it was big Jake. "What are you doing talking to the damn elevator?" Jake asked. "I wasn't talking to the elevator I was humming my favor song and I thought I heard the elevator starting up. But it was just my imagination, the elevators are not moving," said James. Okay, stand guard and keep your god damn eyes open," said Big Jake. Karen could hear bits and pieces of their conversation, but she couldn't make out exactly what was being said.

As soon as Big Jake was gone, James begins pacing back and forth trying to figure out a way to rescue Karen. Danny Stoneberger was walking by and James remembered seeing his file on the desk in the prayer room. "Hey man, did you speak with the Karen today?" James asked. "Yeah man she is a great lady, she's a lifesaver. If I'm ever in a position to help her out, man I would give my right hand to do so," Danny responded. James quickly pulled him into the hallway and told him, today is the day you can give her both of your hands. He told him that Karen was stuck in the elevator and the air circulation wasn't good. Danny became outraged, Karen was his only gleam of hope that he might see daughters and give them the money he saved. "I'm going to kill those stupid motherfuckers, T-bone and Big Jake," said Danny He balled his fist up and punched it in the other hand several times.

It was hard for James to calm Danny down, but he did. "Shut up man, you don't want to put her life in danger do you?" "No," said Danny. "Right now, we need to find a way to save Karen's life. You can deal with them fools later" said James. "Okay, let me think, there must be a way we can get her out of there. I know just how we can do it," said Danny. James anxiously asked how? Danny told him about the air conditioner shaft leading from the public bathroom to the inmates visiting room. It has been used to smuggle drugs into the joint. James had no idea of what Danny was talking about, but was eager to hear the details. Danny agreed to take the risks of rescuing Karen, after all he had nothing to lose.

Before they could put their plain in motion, Big Jake walked up. "What Y'all up to," Big Jake asked? James quickly responded, "nothing Big Jake, we just trying to figure out a plan if the guards from the fourth floor tried to sneak an attack on us." "All right I don't want no double-crossing bullshit going on, because I'll have to kill me some Bitches up in here today." "Who you the hell are you calling a bitch," Danny asked? Trying to restrain for kicking Big Jake's ass, took everything Danny had inside of him. James quickly jumped into the conversation. "He's not talking about us, Danny. He is talking in general man." The look on Big Jack's face told another story. Big Jake wasn't the type of dude to be messed up with. He had been in prison for ten years and pumped enough iron to look like a three-hundred-pound wrestler.

As soon as Big Jake walked to the other end of the floor, Danny ran around to the visitor's bathroom. He went into the first stall and stood on top of the toilet seat and pushed the ceiling panel back. He swung his body back and forth until he was able to leap to the next panel. He crawled over to the air conditioner vent leading to the elevator shaft and with his shank, he unscrewed the screws. It was just enough room for him to slide through the hole in the air conditioner shaft. He crawled a few feet until he reached the elevator. He could see the elevator just below him. He hopped onto the elevator rope, leading to the elevator and climbed down. It took only a few minutes before Danny reached the top of the elevator panel.

Karen could hear noise directly above her. She didn't make a sound because she had no idea who it was. He cut a hole through mental with his shank. It was hot as hell in there, he was sweating all over the place. Once Danny cut a hole in the top of the panel big enough for him to fit through, Karen was relieved to see a friendly face. Danny held on to the sides of the hole as he lowered himself down in the elevator. Karen embraced him for saving her. They both whispered to each other. "I'm so glad to see you, Danny." "I'm glad to see you're doing okay Karen."

Just as they were whispering to each other, on the outside of the elevator Big Jake had returned to James' post. "Where did Danny disappear to?" Big Jake asked. "He didn't say where he was going", James responded. "Something funny is going on between you two," said Big Jake. "Nah man we straight on this riot shit," said James.

Just as James finished talking, Karen sneezed loudly and Jake heard the noise coming from the elevator. "who is in there? Big Jake yelled out."

Shush Danny signal Karen with his index finger while covering her mouth with his other hand. Danny quickly pointed up to the hole in the panel. Danny cuffed his hands so Karen could step up and gain access to the hole. She swung her legs in the air until she was able to lift her body through the hole. Danny couldn't reach the hole without a lift. He told Karen to go down to the third floor and hide in the men's public bathroom. Pull the panel back in place and go into the last stall. "what about you?" she asked. "Don't worry about me, I'll be fine, it's important that you get out of here alive," said Danny.

Karen quickly followed the path leading to the men's bathroom. She found the open panel and hopped down, landing one foot inside the toilet. She stood on the toilet seat and slipped the panel back in place. Then she hurried to the last stall, stoop in a kneeling position on top of the toilet.

No sooner had she closed the bathroom door, when Big Jake and two other inmates, Luke and Snake Man, came charging in the bathroom to inspect their secret panel. Snake Man saw traces of water on the floor leading from the first stall to the last stall. "Hey man someone has been in here," said Snake Man. "Let's check all the stalls, just to be on the safe side," said Luke. "No don't be silly, no one could have gotten pass James at the elevator and we have all the guards on this floor as hostages", said Big Jake. Luke, wasn't taking any chances, he started kicking in the stalls one by one. "Come out – come out whoever you are" yelled Luke. Before he could kick in the last

stall, T-bone came rushing into the bathroom to inform them that the National Guard had arrived. "Come on let's get in place man. If it's a war they want, then it's a war they will get."

Karen's heart was nearly in her hand when Luke started kicking the doors in, her blood rushed to her head. She sat flat on the toilet once they had left out the bathroom. Frighten with fear, she pissed on herself.

Captain O'Hara of the National Guard was in charge, he had his men cut a hole through the fence leading into the prison yard. Then they surrounded the prison, dressed in their riot gear. Captain O'Hara was expecting, to face one of the worst prisoner's takeover in a decade. They quickly moved onto the ground floor of the prison. The civilians had been evacuated upon the sound of the riot alarm earlier.

Captain O'Hara phoned the warden as soon as he and his men were stationed on the ground floor. The warden was relieved to hear his voice. He gave the captain an update on the status of the riot. It was confined to the second and third floors. The guards had the other inmates secured in their cells on the other floors. Since the riot was taking place on the second and third floors, it wouldn't be as bad as Captain O'Hara first thought.

He told the warden to look out the east window and see the national guards posted below his window. The warden put the phone down and went over to the window. Sure enough, the guards were standing out there. He rushed back to the phone and acknowledge their presence. Captain O'Hara gave him strict instructions, go over to the window and break it, then drop the keys down for the stairwell. Switched the elevators on and send them non-stop to the first floor. Then warden followed the instructions Captain O'Hara gave him. The warden went back to his office and sat in his chair, waiting for further instructions from the captain. One of the National Guards posted by the window picked the keys up and ran around to the entrance of the prison and gave them to Captain O'Hara.

Once Captain O'Hara had the keys in hand, he radioed to his

second commander outside the yard gate to get on the bullhorn and try to get the inmates to surrender. All the windows had been broken out on the second and third floor in the correctional guard break room, leaving only the bare iron bars remaining on the windows. T-bone and the other inmates were all gathered around the windows, watching the National Guard position themselves.

The inmates only had makeshift weapons and all the guns were located on the fourth floor with the warden. The second commander shouted out to the inmates "surrender peacefully and no additional charges will be filed against you. If you don't surrender in the next ten minutes, there could be a lot of unnecessary bloodshed." T-bone yelled in response "We have a list of demands we want to be met and we want to speak to the Governor now! If we don't see her here in the next 10 minutes, there's going to be a lot of dead correctional guards. Do you hear me?" The governor's mansion was ten minutes away from U-Horn Prison. The governor had a decoy car at the mansion after an attempt was made on her life.

In a hurried voice, Commander O'Hara phoned the governor and told her they were in the position to storm the second and third floors of the prison. The governor told Commander O'Hara, to do whatever was needed to regain control of the prison.

Seeing the national guardsmen posted around the prison, some of the inmates became jittery and angry about the take-over. Especially, Buster, he was due to be paroled in a week, after spending the last fifteen years of his life behind bars. He had gotten married while in prison to a beautiful young lady named, Christina. During a conjugal visit, they co-created a child. Buster's chest and arm muscles were large, he stood about 6'1 and weighed 270 lbs.

"Motherfucker who put you in charge of deciding my fate. Huh? This dumb shit ain't going to do nothing but get some of us killed or more prison time." Buster said to T-Bone. Big Jake tapped Buster on the shoulders and said, "Punk bitch, this was my idea. So what the hell are you going to do about it?" Before Buster could turn all the way around, Big Jake quickly, wrapped his forearm around Buster's neck from behind and threw him to the floor. Big Jake fell down as well, they began to tussle back and forth. While Big Jake was on top, he punched him in the right eye, causing it to bleed. Buster, shove Big Jake off him with his legs. They both got back on their feet. Buster wiped the blood from his face. They began doing the fight dance, going around in a circle. Big Jake stepped back and threw a "mean" right at Buster's face, Buster duck and he missed. As Buster came up, he inched forward and hit Big Jake with two quick karate chops to the throat. Big Jake grabbed his throat and Buster finish kicking his ass. The inmates had gathered around watching the fight. T-Bone had to pull Buster off of big Jake.

With the distraction from the fight, the National Guard had made their way up the stairwell to the second and third floor. When T-bone and the other inmates looked up, they were staring down the barrels of M-16 guns. All the inmates were ordered up against the wall to be searched. They had to use tear-gas on the prisoners on the second floor and regained control without any incident. The inmates who had weapons on them were handcuffed, along with T-bone. Big Jake had to be taken to the infirmary. Captain O'Hara notified the warden, that the riot was over. The correctional guards had been freed and they put the inmates back into their cells. The warden went into the hallway and pushed the button for the elevator. When the elevator door opened, he found Danny barely breathing, laying on the floor. Danny had just enough energy to whisper to the warden that Karen was in the men's bathroom on the third floor in the last stall. The warden had the guards take Danny to the infirmary for medical care.

He quickly went up to the third floor to rescue Karen. He pushed the bathroom door open and found Karen hysterically shaking in the stall. He took her hand and gently pulled her out the stall and hugged her. He told her that it was over. She was still shaking as they walked towards the elevator. Once inside the warden's office, Karen sat on the black couch and composed herself. The warden got her a glass of water. Then he sat in the brown chair, in front of Karen. He tried to explain, why he didn't try to get her out the elevator. It was prison policy during at riot, to shut the elevators off. If the look she had on her face could have killed him, he would have been a dead man.

Once she wrapped her mind around what she just went through she was ready to get the hell out of there. The warden insisted that she stay a while longer, she needed to fill out some paperwork regarding the riot. Karen told him she would come back another time to fill out the paperwork, she had to get out of there now! After everything she had been through since early morning, her mind was at its breaking point and she might just snap. The warden agreed. Once Karen reached her car in the parking lot, she got in it and drove off like a maniac doing fifty-miles an hour in a 20-miles speed zone.

Back in the prison, the Warden got all the details from Danny about the rescue and he recommended an earlier release date for James. Danny's sentencing came with a mandatory of ten years before he could be considered for parole. One of the correctional guards, who was taken as a hostage, had witnessed the actions of Buster and told the warden. If had not been for Buster taking a stand against the take-over, it could have been a lot of bloodshed. The warden had no idea, how the national guard had caught the inmates by surprise. He was going to contact the governor, to see if Buster could get a pardon, rather paroled.

Karen arrived at her house in twenty minutes. She rushed inside and threw her briefcase down and stretched out on the couch trying to make sense out of her whole day. Was God punishing her or something? This type of shit only happens in the movies, not in real life, she thought to herself. She knew that comment would make Pastor Haywood scratch his head if he had heard it. She went into the bathroom and grabbed some sleeping pills out the medicine cabinet. She took one pill and in last than an hour she was sound asleep. The phone was ringing, but she didn't hear a thing. Karen continued sleeping until the next day.

Karen awakened to the sound of someone pounding on her front door. It was her handyman coming to show her how to use the security system. Just a minute she said to her handyman, then she rushed into the bathroom to refresh and put on her robe. Then she let him in, he took twenty minutes to show her how to operate the alarm system. After he left, Karen checked her answering machine, Jackie had left a message. "Hi, Karen it's me and I'm having the time of my life. I went to a game show in Nigeria called Dial 1-900 –Recycle- A Man and Woman. Girl, it's the funniest thing you'd ever want to see. I was shocked to see men participating. I'll tell you more about it when I come home Friday. My flight arrives at 3:30 pm, please be there to pick me up. Also, see if you can get some tickets for me, you, Roxanne and Janice to go to Mrs. B's Comedy Show at the Oasis. Love you Bye!"

Karen went on the internet to find Gloria's mother's phone number. She had to dial five different Rosetta Brown's before she found the right one. At first, there was some resentment in Rosetta's voice when Karen told her she was calling on behalf of Danny Stoneberger. "I don't want anything to do with that crazy motherfucker," replied Rosetta. "I'm not asking you to do anything for him. I promised him that I would deliver some money he had saved for his daughters. He wants them to know that he still loved them and think about them all the time. I don't think that's asking too much Ms. Brown?" "No it's not asking too much, I'll take any money he has to

offer them. It's been hard for me trying to raise two little girls at 65 years old. And if it wasn't for Danny my, daughter would still be alive. So don't expect me to be damn sympathetic to him." "No ma'am, I don't expect you to be, but maybe one day you might be able to forgive him." They made arrangements for Karen to come by the next day with the money for the girls.

After Karen hung up the phone, she started thinking about James again. Her body chemistry for him was stirring up beyond her control. Hell, she was fantasizing about the man and they only kissed that one time. Karen was doing some soul searching about her attraction to James. She must be out of her damn mind or desperate to want to get involved with a criminal, however, that sensational feeling continued to flow through her body every time she thought of him.

The next morning, Karen went over to Rosetta Brown's house. On the way over there, she kept wondering what Rosetta was going to be like in person. On the telephone, Rosetta seemed like the type that didn't take any shit off no one. Karen rang the doorbell and a heavy set, fair-skinned woman with red streaks in her hair greeted her at the door. Yeah, she fits the "I don't take no shit" description. Karen thought to herself. "Come on in honey and have a seat. Phyllis and Robin come on in the living room, there's someone here to see you," said Rosetta. Two beautiful little girls came out to meet Karen. Phyllis was the spitting image of Danny and from the pictures hanging on the wall, Robin resembled her mother, Karen thought to herself.

"Who is this lady grandma? Phyllis asked her grandma." This is a friend of your daddy and she came to bring you'll something from him. The two girls sat on each side of Karen and asked how was their daddy doing and when was he coming home? Karen told them he was doing fine and there's no telling when he was coming home. However, he thinks of them all the time and he asked her to give them this money, he had saved for them. It was a check for $138.00 dollars. Karen also told them he wanted them to write to him. She gave them each a hug for him, then wrote down his prison address for them. Phyllis and Robin's face brightened with a big smile, knowing their father was still thinking about them.

Rosetta didn't say a word, the expressions on their faces told the story. Rosetta promised to take them to visit their father. Karen left feeling that her mission was accomplished.

Karen went to her office, after leaving Rosetta's house and called the warden. She wanted him to relay a message to Danny Stoneberger, she had delivered the money to his girls and their grandma promised to bring them down there to see him next month. She also left her telephone number for James Washington and Danny Stoneberger to call her if they needed to talk to her doing her visit at the prison.

Warden Jones agreed, he delivered the message as soon as he hung up with Karen. He still felt bad about the ordeal she had endured at his prison. He also informed James that he had spoken to the parole board and the governor. They had no problem with releasing him as early as tomorrow. James felt happy as a kid on Christmas Day. He also thought about what it would feel like making love to Karen for the first time. Then that thought was knocked out his mind, with a reality check that he was a convicted criminal and she probably wouldn't give him the time of day. But he was going to try to at least talk with her. When it was his phone time, he called his home-boy Edwin and told him about his early release. He also wanted Edwin to find out where

Karen lived. James gave Edwin her phone number because he had connections at the phone company.

At eight o'clock a.m., they came to James' cell block and called his name to be released. He took a few personal belongings, but he left everything else to his homey Cocker Roach. Cocker Roach was going to be in there for another five years. James stepped outside the prison gates and threw his hands in the air and shouted, "free at last thank you God." Edwin was there to pick him up. "Hey man, did you get that information on Karen?" "Yeah man, I got the information, who is this bitch anyway?" "Watch your mouth man she ain't no bitch, she's a lady." "On, then who is this lady that's got your screws loose upstairs?" "Man I met her in the joint, she's a psychiatrist and she sent heat waves through my body." Huh, you got to be kidding me; you ain't trying to hook-up, with no damn shrink man." "I know it's something magical about her, I felt it the first time we met. I have to at least give it try. Take me to mom's house and then drive me to her house."

When James' mom laid eyes on him she was grinning from ear to ear. My baby is home, she said. They hugged each other for a few seconds. James had gotten much bigger. "I have a job lined up with your uncle Albert, at Hector's Auto Dealership, his mother said." "Okay mom, I'll go to see him first thing to tomorrow." James hurried back out the door and got into Edwin's car. "All right man, take me there. No first take me to the free client." "Why in the hell do you want to go there?" Edwin asked. "I want to have an. AIDS test done." James replied. Edwin's eyes got big, as he looked over at James strangely. "No man, I didn't get raped in prison. I would have killed someone if they would have tried me. I just want to have all my ducks in a row, so whenever that magical moment happens between Karen and I." "You don't even know if she is going to give you the "time of day" and you're doing all this shit." said Edwin. "Just take me to the damn clinic man," said James. "Alright".

Edwin dropped James off at the clinic. He told James that he will pick him up in an hour and like clockwork, Edwin was on time. Edwin wanted to know what the results of the test. James told him they were negative. Edwin dropped him off at the corner of Karen's house. James got out the car and said he'd wait until she returned home. "Man are you're crazy, there are a lot of "sliders" you can get some play from." said Edwin "I'm not about that no more, man it's time that I become focused in my life." "All right call me if you change your mind." "Bet it up, man." James walked over to the park across from Karen's house. Edwin drove off.

Karen arrived home around three o'clock p.m. She poured herself a drink of rum and coke and sat down on the couch. The drink relaxed her, she decided to take a hot bath and finish unwinding. No sooner had she gotten in the tub, there was a hard knock at the door. She put her robe on. Once she reached the living room, she yelled, "Who is it?" The voice on the other side said, the newspaper man." "I don't want to subscribe to the paper", Karen said." "If you just give me a minute of your time mam, I might be able to change your mind" the voice yelled back. Karen became pissed, who in the hell did this salesman think he was. I made up my mind, she thought to herself.

She snatched the door open and was ready to read this salesman, her eyes nearly popped out, at the sight of James. "Can I have a chance to change your mind miss," he said jokingly. "Of course, how did you find out my address," she asked? "I have my ways. Are you going to invite me in, he asked? He asked "Sure come on, I don't know where my manners are," she replied.

They both went into the house and sat down on the loveseat. She started asking more questions. "When did you get out?" "I was released this morning." "What made you look me up so soon," she asked? "Karen, I'm not going to play games, I'm going to be on the up and up with you. That visit, I had with you in prison left an impression on me that I can't explain. I've never felt for a woman what I feel for you. I don't believe in love at first sight, but I do believe in fate. Once I get myself situated I would like to date you," he said. Karen was shocked and couldn't speak at first. Here was this man that made her "cookie" tingle like crazy, asking to see her on a regular basis. Should she be cautious or live a little dangerously, she thought to herself. "Let's go out on a few dates, let me get to know you on the outside of the prison bars and then we will take it from there," she said. James reached over and placed a gentle kiss on her forehead. There was no resisting on Karen's part. They caressed for a minute, then they got a grip on themselves. They didn't want to move too fast and they didn't just want it to be a sexual thing either.

The next day James went to see his Uncle Albert and got a job as a car salesman. His Uncle Albert was the general manager at Hector's Auto Dealership. He gave James the keys to loaner car to use and a week advance of his salary. Khori was the best salesman, he was assigned to train James. Khori was a single father raising his daughter.

That was the driving force that made him the best car salesman. James needed to start somewhere in the work-force; a car salesman wasn't going to be his future. He called Karen at her job and told her about his new job. She was excited for him. They made plans to go to dinner that night to celebrate after work.

James went to his mother's house and showered and packed an overnight bag just in case he didn't come home. He picked Karen up and they went to dinner that night at a romantic restaurant by the river. They stared into one another's eyes most of the night and held hands. Then they went to Karen's house for a nightcap. It was late, so Karen invited him to spend the night. James was a little reluctant; he didn't want anything to go wrong between Karen and him. Karen teased him about it, I'm not going to rape you, she said. James smiled. He slept on the couch and before morning Karen came out and cuddled up with him.

However, nothing happened sexually until the next night. They could no longer resist the tension of just kissing. They both got into the shower and washed each other's body and James begins nibbling on her breast like a baby. Karen was ready by the time they got out of the shower. She got some whip cream and spread it on his chest and gently licked it off. He spread some on her belly button and other places. Before that magic moment, the both said hold up for a minute. James went into his pants pocket and Karen went into her nightstand, they both retrieved condoms. They fell out laughing. "Great minds think alike," James said. Karen nodded in agreement. Karen asked, by the way, when was the last time you got tested for AIDS, he smiled and said today. Then he put the red condom on.

Then the magic moment was about to happen. His he whispered in her ear, can I make love to you. She smiled and said yes. He hadn't had sex in over three years but he wanted to be gentle as he could possibly be. He opened her legs and slid inside her. Hoping he

could resist from coming too quickly. Karen had the skills, she viewed sex as art and with every stroke she made, she was sexually painting a Picasso. She knew how to make her "cookie" sing and dance at the same time. James could feel every hump she made, she moved like she was pumping air in a tire, with a hand-held pump. He asked her to take it easy on him. She smiled and slowed down a little bit so he could catch his breath. Karen had not had sex in months it was hard for her to keep from climaxing. Karen rolled him over and got on top and began moving back and forth. He grabbed onto her ass while she stroked him like he had never been stroked before. He wanted to have sex all night long, but he couldn't hold back and he started climaxing. He lost all control and started breathing heavy and gasping for air. "Karen oh baby, Karen got damn you're good." They both collapsed afterward and fell asleep in each other's arms.

The next morning, they woke up smiling uncontrollably at each other, then kissed. Before they got started again, they got out the bed and showered together. Had a cup of coffee and a bagel. James told her would call her later. Then they left for work. Karen sat in front of her window at the office looking at the lake across the street. The ripples in the water relaxed her mind and she started thinking about her new sexual relationship with James. If that's what you could call it at this point. She had never engaged in a sexual encounter so soon with any man she had dated. Her motto was, get to know the man, before you get to know his penis. She always had to wait until she knew him long enough, because of the myth, about giving up your "cookie" too quickly and being left with nothing. However, if that did happen, at least you wouldn't have invested all your time and emotions in a man only to be left later down the road. If it didn't work out with James, at least her sexual fantasy about him would have been fulfilled.

Then a small motor boat came along and startled Karen. She snapped out of her daze and asked Maritza to send her nine o'clock client in. As Ms. Jennifer Page entered the room, Karen greeted her with a friendly smile and asked her to have a seat. Jennifer was a small frame woman with thick black hair and cat eye contact lenses. "How are you doing today, Jennifer?" Karen asked. "Fine Doctor." "You can call me Karen if that makes you feel comfortable." "All right." "Is there anything in particular, you want to discuss today Jennifer?" "Karen, my life has gotten a little hectic since my last visit with you. What happened? "It's my family. Greed has destroyed our family. Several years ago, my mother, father and I bought a house together. My father passed away ten years ago, leaving me to foot his share of the mortgage payments and taxes. I worked two jobs to pay the taxes on the house. Even with my medical conditions, I had a heart attack at 39 years old and have been diagnosed with lupus after I had my second child at 25. To make a long story short, my mother went to live with my brother. He convinced her to sell the house. I found out about her trying to sell the house when I received documents from a lawyer. Not over my dead body was I going to sell the house. My brother sent a contractor over to our house to get an estimate for remodeling without my permission. At first, I was going to fight it by hiring a lawyer, but it cost money to retain a lawyer. My daughter told me not to waste my time or money. . My health was more valuable than money and that house. I cried and cried. I couldn't believe what was happening to me.

Here I am 59 years old, looking for somewhere to live. I found a two-bedroom apartment, and moved in it with, my daughter and grandson." Karen explained it's not always easy to adapt to change. She had to look at her pros and cons. Then focus on the pros of her new lifestyle. One of the pros was that she had the money to relocate. She had her daughter and grandson that loved her and God have given her life to start over again. The relationship with her brother and mother is something she would have to work on. Jennifer said she didn't care if she never spoke to him again. She felt betrayed by her mother, but she loves her and hopes that one day their relationship can be mended. Her mother is in her almost ninety-one and Karen told Jennifer she doesn't want to be standing over her grave asking for forgiveness.

Last but not least Karen told her it's not what happens to you in life, it how you react to what happens that makes the world of difference. You can allow it to destroy you, or you can learn from it. If whatever happened to you didn't take you out the game of life, then you can adapt and move on to bigger and better things. Jennifer agreed and that was the end of her therapy sessions. Jennifer made an appointment for her next session. Karen was jotting down notes after her sessions with Jennifer.

Raquel was the ideal fit for Karen's practice, she was friendly, outspoken, and had the skills to run the office in Karen's absence. Not to mention, she was once Karen's client. It had been years since Raquel had been in a healthier and happy relationship. All that changed when she got involved in with Sandy. This was Raquel's first time having a partner who was the same sex. There was something special about Sandy, that peeped Raquel's interest. Even Karen noticed the glow on Raquel's face when she came into work. When Karen asked her what the glow was from, Raquel simply hummed a few of the melodies from Denise Williams song, "I Found Love." Karen nodded her head forward and whispered to herself I'm glad she did.

Another asset, Raquel adds to the practice, is her ability to entertain the clients with her life stories until Karen is ready to meet with them.

Karen has an intern named Maritza, who comes in for four hours a day. She is attending college, to earn her Master's Degree, at night. It was Maritza's husband, Patrick who encouraged her to pursue her Master's Degree after their two children got older. He was a close friend of Karen, that how she was able to get the internship. She was also a great asset to Karen's practice. She talks with the clients who not in the mood for Raquel's bubbly personality.

Mr. Boston, her ten o'clock client, arrived at the office. He was a handsome looking man with salt and pepper hair, hazel brown eyes, and a medium built body. You could tell he took good care of his body in his younger days. Raquel, who is Karen's office manager, told Mr. Boston to have a seat.

Mr. Boston didn't waste any time talking. He had been seeing Karen for the past year. He was having trouble with his penis staying erect and climaxing. He was forty years of age and he had gone to see several doctors about this problem. They couldn't find anything medically wrong, so the doctors determined it was a mental problem." Karen if I don't get my "penis" to act right, I might just lose my wife. I bought her a vibrator and she was insulted. She told me if she wanted a cold hard dick she could go screw a stiff in the morgue. I was only trying to make sure she was satisfied at home. You know how some of us brothers thrive on sex. We feel like king-kong in bed. For the past six months, I've felt like Popeye without my spinach.

Mr. Boston according to all of my notes during our sessions, this problem first occurred when you attempted to have an affair with your secretary Marlen. Whom you described as drop-dead gorgeous and had a body most women wished they had. Only to find out after you got to the hotel and got in bed, that Marlen she had more penis than you had. I think it's been hard for you to live that incident down. Along with the fact, that Marlen has been blackmailing you. The only way you're going to get a fresh start and get your life back on track is to confess to your wife. Blackmailers never go away; in fact, they want more and more. You've already given Marlen several unscheduled raises. You can't fire him because he can "yell" discrimination. However, what you can do, is secretly tape record one of your conversations where he mentions the blackmailing. Then you might have the evidence to terminate him. However, you should consult legal counsel on this.

All right, Karen, I'm going to tell my wife I don't know what is going to happen, it can go either way. She can accept my mistake or she can leave me. But at least I can move on one way or another. And I will contact my attorney about getting proof of the blackmailing. I might be able to prosecute Marlen if she pushes the issue. He made an appointment with Karen for next month. Karen called it a day she jotted down her notes from the sessions and went home early.

Chapter 6

Michael pondered with the thought of taking a leave of absence from the fire department, indefinitely, even though this was his only means of income. Nevertheless, there was no way he could function up to standards, in the mental condition he was in. Who in the world would want a depressed fireman trying to rescue them from a five-story burning building? Can you imagine a fireman reaching a suicidal jumper and decide to commit suicide, himself?

Michael went to speak with a counselor at the "Employee Assistance Program, "to be evaluated. He told the "E.A.P". Counselor part of his situation. He left out the part, though about being arrested. The counselor wrote his commanding officer a memo, requesting that Michael takes a leave of absence, indefinitely, for personal reasons.

Michael went to the Bonanza Bank and took out five-thousand dollars. He saved this money for a rainy day; however, he had no idea his problems would pour in like a storm. Michael had only one good friend, named Troy. He phoned Troy at work and asked him to drop by his condo after he got off. Troy agreed. Troy arrived at Michael's condo around 5:30 p.m. Michael greeted him with a half- smile on his face and they did a brotherly embrace. Troy was stunned at Michael's unsettled demeanor. Michael had always been an upbeat spirited person, but now he was marching to a downbeat tune.

Michael started telling Troy about the shit he was going through. You could hear the frustration in every word he uttered. Troy listened with much empathy, but at the same time, he was wondering if he should drop a bomb on Michael's already explosive life. He thought about telling him, that it was Charlotte who called his job at the computer company and informed them of his arrest. Troy decided to wait until Michael got himself together mentally because that could send him over the edge.

Troy knew one day, that Michael would run into a woman that he couldn't buy with material things. Even when he didn't agree with Michaels' actions, he didn't poke his nose his personal life. When Michael dumped his cousin Charlotte, a month before their wedding, was a hard pill for Troy to swallow. This was the one time Troy did poke his nose in and told Michael how pissed-off he was. For a while, it put a strain on their friendship, Troy didn't speak to Michael for a month. Now Troy felt Michael was reaping some of the pain he had sowed.

Michael asked Troy to house-sit his condo until he returned

from Trevenor City. Troy was staying at home with his mother assisting her financially, so it wasn't a big deal to move into Michael's condo for a while.

Michael arrived at Rain-Bow Train Station. He left his Cadillac parked at the train station garage storage. He purchased his train ticket and anxiously waited for the six o'clock train to Trevenor City, his hometown. He began pacing back and forth, on the sidewalk, in his tight-fitting blue jeans, T-shirt and baseball cap. The train couldn't get there quick enough to take him out of Pie County. His life had turned into a living nightmare. He felt as though he was no longer in control of his destiny and fate had dealt him a cruel hand in hearts.

His mind was clogged with evil thoughts of Jackie, along with the agony he felt for her in his heart. He wasn't mentally equipped to deal with these type of problems. He had lost his appetite and became jittery at every sound he heard. He was on the edge of a nervous breakdown. Thoughts of suicide raced through his mind like a siren none stop. His self-conscience wouldn't allow him to act out on those suicidal thoughts. How could he have been such a fool to let a woman get that close to his heart? Here he was in the prime of his life, at the

age of thirty and close to losing his mind over a bitch. Michael realized he needed someone to pick him up at the Trevenor Train Station. He phoned his mother and told her to pick him from the train station. She agreed.

The whistle finally blew for boarding the train. Michael hurried aboard to get the last seat in the back next to the window. Once he sat down, he pierced his brown eyes down the aisle, looking in the daze, hoping no one would sit next to him, especially a woman. That's the last thing in the world he needed now. The train started moving slowly, no one took the empty seat next to him.

Michael waited until nighttime, and then he pulled a pint of gin from his coat pocket along with a little coke he had folded in a dollar bill. He sipped on the gin and took a small hit of cocaine along the way to Trevenor City. Michael had not indulged with cocaine since he was twenty-one. He didn't sleep a wink. He started thinking back to when he first met Jackie—how he had given up alcohol, just to please her. Now that bitch has him indulging in his old habits again.

"Women are the cause of all men's problems." "You try to please them and they don't appreciate a damn thing." This was a discussion two male passengers were having a couple seats in front of Michael. Michael moved up a seat, to get closer to listen because that shit was sounding good to his ears. They were discussing exactly what was on his mind. "What's up bro, I couldn't help but overhear Y'all conversation back there. I hope Y'all don't mind if I join in?" Michael asked. "No my man, help yourself", one of them replied. Michael was on cloud nine, anything was liable to come out of his mouth at this point. "Man I don't know why women try to dog you out. I was in love with this hoe; I would have given her the world if she wanted it. The only thing I wanted in return was a little quality time. Now Y'all tell me, is that a small price to pay for a man who wants to give you the world? Y'all know those "Ms. Its', who think they are God's gift to men just because they got a good split between their god damn legs," said Michael. The men burst out laughing loudly. "Shit," Michael said.

One of the other men started talking next. "Man I know exactly what you are talking about. I was out there selling drugs eight hours a day, for this bitch, hustling my ass off. Dodging bullets like I was superman and shit. Just so she could have the finer things in life. I ain't got no high school diploma, so there was no way I could get me one of those fifty-thousand-dollar-a-year legal jobs. But I got mine in the streets. I got locked up for a year and a half; jail comes with the territory. I got out of jail, all happy and shit. I thought I would surprise my baby, so I didn't tell her the date I was getting out. I arrived at the house and got a surprised my damn self. That hoe had a baby from someone else and he was living in the house I had brought. I wanted to beat the shit out of her. Instead, I cussed her ass out like she had stolen something. Hell, she did steal something, she stole my god damn heart. I walked out that door, got in my car and drove away. But if she had been my wife, I would have whipped her ass and his ass good". The two men busted into laughter again, but Michael remained quiet this time.

The guy had struck a nerve in him, a fifty-thousand-dollar nerve. Michael became outraged, and he jumped up and shouted "Y'all ain't in the same category as me. I had a legal job making that kind of money. But the sad part about me, I acted out on those stupid emotions. I'm going back to my seat, shit. Y'all can't help me and I can't help Y'all"

Just then the train came to a sudden halt in Trevenor City. Michael got up and looked at the two men and shook their hands. "Good luck in the woman's market, "he said as he got off the train. Michael looked like someone had shit on his face, his eyes were bloodshot red. His breath smelled of a foul odor along with his body. He tried to act normal when he approached his mother, Ruby. But she could look at her son and tell he was in some type of trouble. He had a distant look of worriation on his face. His mother hugged him and asked 'how was everything going". Michael causally lied, "Fine, I just wanted to come home and visit my favorite lady in the whole wide world." His mother replied, "Come on don't try to pull my leg with that lie; It's your mama you're talking to, not a stranger, son. I know you better than you know yourself".

"Mom it's a long story and I'm not in the mood to discuss it now." "Alright, you can tell your father whatever you want to about why you are visiting. But I hope this has nothing to do with your job at the computer company. Your father would lose his cool if you lost that job. Does it son?" "Damn-it! Mom, didn't I just say I don't want to discuss it. Hell, I'm grown and I don't have to account to anybody, including you. I take care of myself now!"

His mother's first reaction was to slap the shit out of her so-called grown son. Michael had never cursed at his mother before. "I'm sorry mom, I don't know what got into me." "It's okay baby".

At that point, she knew something was seriously wrong with him.

They picked up his luggage and drove home. They sat in the car like mummies; no one made the slightest sound or a movement except for driving.

As they pulled into the driveway, Michael could see his father's slim body frame through the screen door. Michael's stomach balled up into a knot at the sight of his father. How was he going to explain to his father that he might lose his computer programing job? Michael was a success story out of the Ida B, Wells Housing Projects.

Michael finished high school and went to Northwest Trade School to learn how to repair and install computer programs. He received a grant from the government for low-income families, otherwise, he wouldn't have been able to afford the courses. Michael's sister Tramese worked at the State Attorney's Office and his brothers, Lamar and Skeeter had good jobs as correctional officers at the county jail. But Michael's father thought highly of his job than his brothers or sister's jobs. In his father's eyes, Michael had made it big because his job required him to use his mind.

Michael and his mother entered the house. His father grabbed him in a bear hug. "So how are things in the computer world, son?"

"Fine, Dad everything is coming along just great. I decided to take a mini-vacation to visit my family. It's been a year since I last saw you all. I miss mom's juicy fried chicken and her homemade biscuits." "That's fine son. I'm glad to have you home for a short time. We can catch up on the family happenings." Ruby stood in the hallway with tears in her eyes. How could she stand there and watch her son lie because he was afraid of disappointing his father? Michael should have been man enough to tell his father the truth, whatever the truth was.

Ruby started feeling guilty about the psychological impact placed on her children because she stayed married to their father. Michael is the oldest, therefore he witnessed more of his father abused than his sister and brother. Michael grew-up watching his father behave like a lunatic.

Every Friday evening was the "main event." His father would come home drunk as a skunk and find something to argue about. His mother would usher the kids into their bedroom because she knew "Action Joe" the nickname she gave their father was on the scene. Joe thought verbally abusing Ruby was the only way to get his point across. He always started cussing like an insane man about the little things. It was such a routine since he always stated the same damn line. "If a man works all got damn week and can't come home to some peace and quiet, he ain't a man at all."

She would try to calm him down by agreeing with every word he said, no matter how stupid he sounded. One time, he asked Ruby to fix him a peanut butter and jelly sandwich. He pitched a bitch because she put the jelly on the wrong side of the bread. Now come on, what difference did it make what side the jelly was on? If you flipped it over, the jelly would be on top instead of the bottom. He refused to eat it, she gave the sandwich to the children. He ordered her to make him another one.

Her patronizing his stupidity only made matters worse. He would accuse her of making fun of him whenever she agreed with him. He would get in front of Ruby's face and yell, "Don't give me that bullshit, I'm sick and tired of your ass! If you don't watch yourself, I'm going to walk out on you and your kids. Where in the hell would you be then? Up shit creek without a paddle. You need me baby, I don't need you." Those words would burn Ruby up, and she wanted to say, "Leave, Motherfucker! Who's stopping you? Certainly not me." However, she needed him financially because she didn't work. Throwing some of his clothes outside the door, crossed her mind.

However, she was too afraid of what he might do to her physically if she did. The doors in the housing projects were so close and the walls so thin, that everybody always knew what went on in everyone else's household. Onetime, Joe did carry out his threat of leaving Ruby. He came home on a Friday after work, packed his clothes and told Ruby he wasn't putting up with her shit anymore. Ruby was lost for words. She followed him to his car, begging him not to leave her and the kids. How could he do something like this to her, he was the only man she had ever been with sexually. "What about the bills? she asked him."

He just smiled at her, as he put the key into the ignition and said, "I'll see what I can do." He drove off. Rumor had it, that he left her for a younger woman who worked as a stripper at the One Leg Up Strip Club. Rent was due, as well as the other household bills. Joe left her high and dry. Ruby was mad as hell! She could have shot his ass if she had a gun. She went back in the house and began crying for a few minutes, then she realized all her wasted tears weren't going to pay her bills.

Ruby sat down in the wooden chair at her kitchen table and wondered how different her life might have turned out, if she had the courage and faith like her older sister, Althea She held her head down and took her right hand across her face and begin to scratch her forehead. She started reminiscing back to when they were teenagers and Althea told her about this preacher she had heard on television while babysitting the Wellington's nine-month-old son. Althea said she was shocked when she first heard and saw the preacher on television. The Wellingtons were one of the wealthiest white families in Mobile, Alabama, and preacher they were watching on television was Rev. Ike a black man. Althea had never heard of Rev. Ike until that day.

During a casual conversation, Mr. Wellington told Althea, that there were a few of Rev. Ike's messages that impacted their lives. The first one was, "the best way to help the poor is not to become one"; the second one was, "self-image is your net worth"; the third one was, "a quote from the scripture- money is the root of all evil, in reverse lack of money is eviler and the last quote was, "God wanted them to live a life of abundance, not poverty". Once they learned from Rev's Ike's messages on how to view God differently than the way they were taught in church, their whole world changed financially. That conversation with Mr. Wellington along with listening to Rev's Ike's message resonated within Althea's mind.

Althea knew the day would come when she would become a millionaire. Althea left home right after finishing scratch her high school. She took the money she had saved from babysitting the Wellington's son and bought a one-way ticket to New York. She had a place to live and a job lined-up. She moved in with her Leon and his wife. Uncle Leon had a job lined-up at MCM one of the largest record labels as a receptionist. Within two years at MCM Althea met and married one of the hottest music producers named Yaytrackz, his legal name was Lewis Multimore. Although Yaytrackz was a millionaire, Althea had skills, she was a songwriter. Together, they became a powerhouse team, they won 2 Grammies.

As Ruby came back to reality while sitting at the table, she realized Althea's courage and unshakable faith came from Rev. Ike messages "God wanted her to live a life of abundance not struggles", she had heard at the Wellingtons house.

As much as she dreaded calling Althea, she was left with no choice. She sucked up her pride and contacted her for some financial assistance. Althea didn't ask a lot of questions about what she needed the money, she made one statement, "so Joe finally came through on his threat of leaving you." Ruby responded, "un huh." Ruby knew she was in for a little lecturing from Althea. She needed Althea's money, therefore, she had no other choice but to listen to her philosophy.

How every woman should be financially equipped to take care of the household with or without a man. So when shit like this happens, no one has to now your god damn business, but you, God and anybody else you decide to tell. She also told Ruby, she needed to get off her ass and stop depending on a man, even if he is her husband. To go take up a trade or get a job. That was the only way she was going to take control of the direction her life was going in. No one should be in control of destiny or your happiness except God and you. Ruby agreed and thanked Althea for agreeing to wire her the money and for the advice.

Althea wired Ruby the money she needed and a little extra to tie her over for six months. A week after her discussion with Althea, Ruby enrolled in the local college and went after her dream of becoming an R.N. Becoming a registered nurse was her dream before she married Joe and had kids. She had taken some nursing courses before she married Joe. She put her dream on the back-burner and focused on her family.

A few months went by before Joe called Ruby begging to come back home and asking for her forgiveness. She made him sweat for a week before telling him he could come back home. She forgave him but told him she would never forget what he did. She continued pursuing her dream. Joe tried to discourage her, by saying she was too old to be going to college. He would complain about the little things, while Ruby was trying to study. She didn't let his negative comments or behavior stop her. Eventually, Joe realized there was nothing he could do or say that was going to stop Ruby from fulfilling her dream. He accepted the fact that she was going to become an R.N. She finished the nursing program and became a Registered Nurse and they moved out the housing projects.

After reflecting back on her life with Joe and the mental scars her children had endured, she wiped the tears from eyes and went into the living room to join Michael and Joe.

Listening to them reminiscing about the good times from the past had stirred up years of rage that had been concealed within her. She jumped up and started yelling at the top of her lungs. "Stop! Stop! Stop! I knew the day would come when I would no longer fear death motherfucker! The buck stops here now! I sat back like a puppet on a string and watched your dysfunctional behavior as a husband corrupt my household. You're so god damn stupid, that you can't see that your son is in some kind of trouble. He would prefer to lie to you than to stand up to you like a man." Ruby yelled. They had never heard Ruby use that tone of voice except when Joe was drunk. They were speechless for a few moments. Then Michael asked in a humble voice, "Mom are you alright." "No, son tell us what is wrong?" Michael started talking. "Dad, I was sitting here pretending everything was okay because I was afraid of disappointing you. I was on the edge of a breakdown; my whole world has crumbled before my eyes. I almost lost my job at the computer company because I was arrested for raping and beating up Jackie."

Ruby dropped to her knees and cried out "oh God what has happened to my son"? She had a look of disbelief on her face. His father's eyes popped open like a blowfish. The room was filled with silence. You could have heard a pin drop. Michael's father never cried in front anyone before, but he cupped his hands to face, broke down and cried like a baby. Tears poured from his eyes onto the floor. Joe held his head up and ushered Michael to come over, he threw his arms around him tightly and told him, never to fear any man including him. "I'm so sorry you had to go through this pain alone."

Ruby felt as though a knife had been removed from her heart.

She gasped for air. Michael sat down and told them all the details of what he had done to get arrested. The next day, Ruby made arrangement for the entire family to attend therapy sessions. One of the doctor's she worked with had a friend named Willie who was a therapist and, they agreed to meet with the family.

During their s therapy session, Willie asked Joe to describe his childhood. After listening to Joe, He uncovered the cause of the pain and suffering the entire family had endured for years. Joe grew up watching his father abuse his mother and he repeated the same abusive behavior in Ruby's life. Michael watched his father's abusive behavior towards his mother and he afflicted that same abusive behavior on Jackie. Joe sat back in his seat, speechless. At first, it was hard for him to accept responsibility for his negative behavior as a husband and father. Willie asked, everyone, to leave out the room except Joe and Ruby. He asked Joe a few soul-searching questions. "Did you add joy or pain, in your family life? Did you realize, you were your son's first teacher, on how to love and treat a woman? You are supposed to set the bar for the type of qualities, your daughter should look for in a man. How high or low did you set the bar?" the therapist asked. Joe had no answers, those questions never crossed his mind. All he could do was hold his head down and moved it from side to side. Willie told him, it's never too late to move forward in a positive direction with his family. He asked Ruby, did she think Joe's dysfunctional behavior as a husband and a father, was normal? Ruby shook her head no, with tears in her eyes. Joe glanced at Ruby and that's when he realized the severity of the pain he had caused in her life.

Willie asked the other family members to come back inside. Joe had something he wanted to say to them. Joe stood up and begin apologizing for his negative behavior, he displayed while they were growing-up. He had no idea of how it impacted their lives. He got down on his knees, in front of Ruby and took her hand and asked her to forgive him. She was the best thing that happened in his life, besides his children. Ruby stood up and ushered Joe to get off his knees. She accepted his apology and they hugged for a long time. This was the first time, three of his adult children had ever seen their father remorseful for his actions. Willie requested to meet with Michael, alone the next day. He recommended that Michael continue his therapy when he returned to Pie County. Michael agreed. Joe and Ruby made a follow-up appointment with Willie.

Chapter 7

In a few days, Michael would be returning home to Pie County. He gained a few pounds and felt better about himself as a man. He phoned Troy and told him he was returning home sooner than he had told him. Troy figured since Michael sounded cheerful, it was a good time to tell him that Charlotte was the person that called the computer company and almost got him fired. Michael paused on the phone for a moment and responded calmly, "that is water under the bridge now." Troy also, informed him that a notice from the court came in the mail for him. Michael told him he would deal with that when he returned home. After hanging up the phone with Troy, he felt like a jackass for stalking Jackie in the shopping mall and going to Karen's house.

The next day, Michael's cousin Balinda called his mother's house because she heard he was in town. During his conversation with Balinda, she told Michael that she was performing at the Oasis Lounge in Pie County the weekend coming. She offered to send him some free tickets to her show. Michael gladly accepted since this was the same Oasis Lounge that started the torch to his life with Jackie. Balinda said she would send the tickets through Fed-Ex to make sure he got them in time. When the tickets arrived, he mailed them to Jackie anonymously.

The week went by fast for Karen. She had someone new in her life and she couldn't wait to share her good news with Jackie. She went to the airport Friday afternoon to pick up Jackie. Her flight was scheduled to arrive at 3:30, it arrived on time. Karen anxiously waited for Jackie to exit off of the plane.

When Jackie stepped off the plane and walked towards the gate Karen noticed a radiant glow on her face. Even Jackie's smile shined with joy. "Hey sis, Karen shouted as she held up her hand." Jackie hurried over there and they both hugged. "So I see that trip did you a lot of good," said Karen. "Yes, indeed, it was just what the doctor ordered." They got in the car and Jackie told her about the trip. "Girl, I told you about the game show, but that wasn't the best part of my trip."

Jackie told Karen how her trip to Africa helped to enrich her spirit and soul, so much she intended to take another trip next year with her. It's a beautiful sight, that everyone should see, at least once in their lifetime. Not only was the sights beautiful, she had a life-changing experience while visiting Bunbonayili a village in Ghana.

She met an elder named, Kwowada. As Jackie was walking in the village, Kwowada grabbed her hand and invited her to come into the hut. At first, Jackie was a little reluctant, but she followed her into the hut. Kwowada told Jackie to sit, there was no modern day future in the hut. Jackie set on a piece of beautiful bright yellow cloth that lay upon the ground.

What Jackie didn't know was that Kwowada was known as the woman who had seeing eyes. Although Jackie's black eye had almost faded into her complexion. There was still a small dark trace outlining underneath her eye.

Kwowada took Jackie's hands and placed them on top of her hands. Kwowada closed her eyes and begin speaking to Jackie. She told her the scar you are wearing underneath your eye, is the evidence of the evil spirit that our ancestors had to digest once they were taken into slavery. For they learned to confuse the spirit of love with the evil spirit violence by causing pain to their young by hitting them to correct what is supposed to be a natural way of growth. Just like you crawl before you walk, you make sounds before you say words, that's a natural order of growth. Once the beating starts, then the young one's spirits are broken, and they grow into broken people who don't know how to love. They are taught to solve conflict through some form of violence. If they have no money, they go out and rob, causing pain to others. If they are hurt, they hurt those who close to them.

She told Jackie to close her eyes and then she asked her how many times did your mother or father tell you they loved you while you were coming of age? Jackie was shocked, as she reflected on her upbringing. her parents didn't say I love you. Tears started to run down Jackie's face. Then Kwowada told her to open her eyes and she gave her a big hug.

She told Jackie, the one who created us, lives within us and you must align your spirit with nature in order to renew your mind. Only nature, operates according to the way the creator intended it to. The ocean shares its waters with the sea animals, the sky shares its space with those who were given wings to fly as well as with sun and the moon.

You must search your soul, for the answers to find the true meaning of love. Find forgiveness, for the one, whose wounded spirit, caused the scar upon your face, for he too is confused about love. Forgiveness unclogs the mind and breathes life into the heart. Kwowada and Jackie walked out the hut and all the women in the village were gathered in a circle. Kwowada walked Jackie into the middle of the circle and each one of the women embraced her with a big hug and a kiss on the cheek and said, I love you. She thanked Kwowada and Kwowada told her to remember the one that created you lives within. They hugged. Jackie left the village with a new perspective about love. She felt a sense of wholeness as a woman. She would never forget that powerful experience. When Karen finished, her about Jackie's experience with Kwowada, she had goosebumps. "Enough about my trip, I see you have a glow on your face. So girl, something good must have happened to you while I was gone. Because you haven't looked this happy in a long time," said Jackie "Come on, don't go there, Karen replied. They both started laughing loudly and had to restrain themselves.

Karen dropped Jackie off at her apartment complex and told her they couldn't get any tickets to Mrs. B's Comedy Show. Jackie was disappointed. She loved comedies shows, especially when the comedian is great. Jackie went into the apartment. She was exhausted from the long flight from Africa. She phoned Roxanne to see if she could get tickets. Roxanne's daughter told her she wasn't home. Jackie left a message for Roxanne to call her when she returned home. Jackie took a hot bath, then she relaxed on the couch.

How was she going to get her life back on track? She was no

longer afraid of Michael, in fact, he still could make her stomach tie in knots whenever she thought about their intimate moments. It's funny how the negative actions of someone you love, hurt so bad and at the same time the good memories you shared feel so good, Jackie thought. Then she thought about what Kwowada had said about. She got her knees and prayed that God helps her to find forgiveness for him. She also prayed that God helps him learn the meaning of love.

Jackie went downstairs to the mailbox; she knew her mailed had piled up. She took the stack of mail back to her apartment and begin opening them. There was a red envelope that caught her attention, she opened it up and there were six tickets for Mrs. Bs' Comedy Show. Jackie was excited because Mrs. B was one of the hottest comedians around. Also, the show was sold out two days after the tickets went on sale. She telephoned Rosanne, Janice, and Karen and told them to cancel all their plans for Saturday night because they were going to the Oasis Lounge. You could hear the excitement in their voices. Jackie had no idea who mailed her the tickets, but she was thankful to whoever did.

Michael arrived back in Pie County knowing the real meaning of manhood as well as the value of a woman. He drove to his condo and Troy was there relaxing. They small talked and Michael told him the entire story of his ordeal back home. As Troy sat there listening, he heard a different sound in Michael's voice. It sounded humble. Michael had finally come to grips with whom he was. Troy wanted to stay there until the end of the month. Michael had no problem with that. He went into the master bedroom to unpack his clothes, when he opened the drawer to put them away, he saw a picture of him and Jackie on the beach in the Bahamas. That picture brought back a lot of happy memories. He sat down on the bed and picked the phone up to call her, and then he put the phone down. He couldn't do it. He wondered if she would ever speak to him again.

Saturday came and the girls went to Latoyia's Magic Touch Hair Salon to get the hook-up for the comedy show. Janice got a new sassy short haircut, Jackie got a French roll, Karen being easy going got a wash and ponytail and Roxanne got a wrap. When Latoyia got through working her magic fingers on their hair, they all looked like "new money."

The big night at the Oasis Lounge was finally here. Janice volunteered to pick them up. Janice had on her jean bell-bottom pants suit, Roxanne wore her red wraparound dress, Jackie had on her sleekly forest green, spaghetti strap dress and Karen wore her purple two-piece mini skirt set. They were all dressed "to kill."

"I know you girls want to see some fine hammer knockers tonight?" Said Karen. "We show do," replied Jackie, Roxanne and Janice. "Well, Mrs. B is opening her show with an all-male-review." She is probably using them to go along with her theme "What You See Is Not What You Get," said Karen. "I know that's right," said Janice. That's like going to the meat market and purchasing a sirloin steak and getting the steak home only to find out it had gone bad in the middle, then to top that off the damn meat was on sale so you can't take it back. Now you are left with two choices, either throw the meat away or try to salvage the good portion of the meat. That sirloin steak is just like some men, who are holding on to dysfunctional childhood issues. You can leave his ass or try to work "with his good qualities," said Jackie. The girls started laughing silly after that remark. They arrived at the Oasis Lounge and parked.

As they were walking towards the entrance, Jackie saw Natascha who was her roommate when they attended college. They embraced each other with a big hug. It has been years since they last saw each other. They small talked for a few minutes before Jackie asked her what was she doing at the Oasis Lounge because Natascha had attended seminary school. Natascha laughed at the question before responding. "Just because you work for God doesn't mean you can't enjoy yourself. I have a non-profit organization called G.S.M. (Great Single Mothers) and once a month a few of us go out on the town Tonight I brought Varcia, Shywyona, and Qiana with me, they needed a stress release moment. The other reason I'm at the Oasis Lounge is to support my childhood friend Mrs. B, she sent me tickets to the show." They exchanged telephone numbers and agreed to keep in touch.

"Come on let's go in so we can get a good look at something we can't have but can touch," said Jackie. "Girl! You're too much for me," said Janice. They arrived just in time for the all-male-review. They got seats dead center in the front row. Natascha, Varcia, Shywyona, and Qiana were seated at the table next to them. When the men came out, Varcia and Shywyona had their dollar bills ready. Natascha and Qiana were more reserved but enjoyed what they were looking at. When Black Stallion started dancing next to their table, Varcia put her dollar bill in Black Stallion crotched and Shywyona slapped him on his ass and put a dollar between the crack of his ass.

"Ooh honey; bring your fine self over here, so I can spank that ass. I know your lady is happy every time you get in the bed with her. I can see that just from the bulge in the front of your gee-string, said Karen. "Karen girl, you ain't shame?" asked Janice. "Shame of what! I'm here to have a good time; I'm not looking to take him home with me. Go on girl and squeeze the cheese! It's not going to bite you. You might just like what you feel" Karen told Janice. "What the hell, come on over here Mandingo," said Janice. "That's it girl, grab that fine ass-butt", said Karen." "Girl you're crazy," said Roxanne. "Girl that's how men describe our ass," said Karen.

Now it's time for Mrs. B.'s Show and I'm fired up, said Janice. MC Tuff Love introduced Balinda aka Mrs. B. and the applause from the audience was overwhelming. She strolled across the stage in her hot red one-piece, shear jumper suit. Her hair was in dreads. Looking sassy and sexy as usual. "How's everybody doing tonight?" asked Mrs. B. "Fine" the audience responded. "Before I get started tonight, I would like to send a" shout out" to my favorite cousin Michael Sims sitting over there in the back corner." At the sound of those words Karen, Janice and Roxanne all turned and looked at Jackie. Jackie stared back at them with a so-what gesture. Then they glanced around the room to see if Mrs. B. was talking about the same Michael they knew. Sure enough, there he was sitting his ass across the room, in his black silk Italian suit at a table with Troy. It was hard at first to recognize him with his beard. In fact, if it wasn't for Troy sitting at the table with him, the girls wouldn't have recognized him at all.

Mrs. B continued, "now let's get down to business. Are you ready to have a good time? Usually, I start off talking about men and believe me there is a lot of shit I can say about men. Hell I've been married to one for thirty-five years and I earned a PH.D. –Please-Help Deliver me before I hurt him. Killing him was never an option, I had too much money to lose along with my freedom. In prison, I would have been just another broke sister with a number."

The ladies were enjoying the show and laughing harder than they laughed in a long time. Michael sat glancing over at Jackie throughout the show. Right before intermission, Jackie cut her eyes across the room at Michael and their eyes met at the same time. Jackie made an upward gesture towards the door. Michael pointed his index finger in the same direction and she nodded her head yes. I need to go outside for some fresh air and get a grip on myself, said Jackie. Roxanne, Janice, and Karen threw their hands up acknowledging her leaving.

Michael waited a few minutes before he left his table. Jackie was leaning against Janice's car, as Michael approached her. She didn't know what the hell she was doing out there, but her heart told her to go outside. Michael stood directly in front of her and asked if she could ever find it in her heart to forgive him. "Jackie I know I don't have the right to ask this of you, but in everyone's lifetime, they've done some hurtful things to someone else. The sad part is, you can't take it back or erase it. For the first time in my life, I had someone special to share it with and I acted like a jackass and destroyed it." Jackie sat back, teary-eyed and listened to Michael who was also crying as he was talking. Part of her wanted to grab him and say yes baby I forgive you, but something inside wouldn't let her do it.

She Jackie stood there speechless at first with her arms folded, staring into Michael's eyes. "Michael as good as that sounds and as mad as I was, I can't give you an answer right now. It's going to take some time, but I'll give you a call in the near future." Michael's face lit up with a smile of joy at least she didn't close the door of hope on him.

They went back into the club and sat at their separate tables.

The girls looked at Jackie then glanced over at Michael and shook their heads. Jackie just smiled back at them. She and Michael shared glances throughout the night. They went back inside just in time to hear Mrs. B. finale routine.

Let me tell Y'all a story about shit. Shit is my favor cuss word because we all go through some kind of shit in our lifetime. Some big shit, little shit, and last but not least some stupid shit but at the end of the day shit sums it up, that's what it is shit! Now most of us, not all of us, have fucked over father-time and father-time ain't something to be fucked with. If you are working a dead-end job, over 30, and living from paycheck to paycheck, then you fucked over father-time. One thing about father-time, it will leave your ass, right where you are struggling and complaining. Hell, I know, I use to complain about God not giving me an opportunity to use my talent. I prayed and nothing happened. I prayed again and again, nothing happened. I got in a quiet place and the spirit told me to get off my ass and make something happen. That is exactly what I did, here I am today the number one comedian and all my books are on the Best Sellers list. I learned to use the shit God gave me since birth, which is my god damn mind. This shit has no limitations and just like Star Trek, that shit can take you places you've never been. Use it or lose it! So family, don't settle for any negative shit that shows up in your life. Hold on a minute, sir stand up, no come up here on stage, that t-shirt you have on has been bothering the hell out me all night long." The man was wearing one of those Black History t-shirts with the faces of great black folks. "I know you're not using your shit because right in the middle of these people, you should have a picture of your god damn self. Don't you think you're great?" The man nodded his head yes. The audience laughed. Then she pulled out a hundred-dollar bill, handed it to the man and told him to get a t-shirt made with the same great black folks and put his picture in the middle. The audience clapped.

On a personal note, I'm a grandmother now, ain't that some shit, I have three grandsons, named Jermaine, Jeremiah, and Columbus. They keep my ass hustling like hell but I love that shit all the way to the bank and I love them too." Please stop by the table and purchase copies of my Best Seller books "What's Your Alibi, God's Every Day Celebrities and Fight the Power Be, and The Melodies of Love" along with copies of my DVD's? The audience clapped. "Until next time family, I hope you enjoyed this shit today. It's been real." The audience stood to their feet and gave Mrs. B. a standing ovation. She walked off the stage and over to her for sending him the tickets. She told him to give her a call, so they could catch up on life. He agreed.

Michael had nothing to lose as he strolled over to Jackie's table to ask if he could give her a ride home. Although Jackie needed closure with Michael she was not ready to be alone with him in a car. She told him no thanks. He smiled and said he understood. She told him they could meet for breakfast tomorrow, at her favorite restaurant, Carolyn & Bernal's Good to the Last Bite Restaurant, they have the best chef in Pie County, his name is Reggie. She told Michael he could give her an all in the morning. He agreed.

All the girls just stared at him, however, Karen asks if she could speak to him outside. Michael and Karen walked outside. Karen asked him if had gotten any professional help for his anger issue. He told her that he had gone to counseling and he intends to find a good therapist in Pie County for follow-up therapy. He asked her if she could recommend one to him. She had a strange look on her face and asked him was he serious. He laughed and told her he was. She had a good friend who was a great therapist. She gave Michael, the therapist name, and number. She still had her reservations about him, getting involved with her sister. She told him if he ever laid one hand on her sister, what she would do to him. Michael chuckled to himself, threw his hands up and said, "I still loved Jackie and I promise you I wouldn't do anything to harm her again."

As Michael was walking away, he was thankful, he didn't do anything to Karen that day he broke into her house and made her count from 100- to 1. They went back inside to join Jackie, Roxanne, Janice, and Troy. Everyone walked outside together. It was a little uncomfortable for Janice and Roxanne, they were the ones who had called the police on Michael. There were no ill feelings from him. Troy and Michael said goodnight to the ladies and got into their car. The ladies got into Janice's car and drove off. "So Jackie what are you going to do about Michael.", asked Roxanne. Silence filled the air at first. Karen looked over at Jackie waiting for an answer. Janice jumped in, "girl the choice is yours. I will not think any less of you as a friend or a woman if you took him back. People do make mistakes, hell I know I did and Peter forgave me."

Jackie still didn't answer the question. She knew in order to move forward in her life, she had to forgive him but not forget the ordeal he put her through. She remembered the conversation she had with Kwowada, that forgiveness is the key that unlocks the door to find love with someone new. Too, often women and men don't forgive each other, and take that unforgiving luggage into their next relationship or recycle it in the same relationship, and they don't grow. Janice dropped all the ladies off and drove home where Peter was waiting for her.

The next morning Michael called and Jackie and they met at Carolyn & Bernal's Good to the Last Bite Restaurant for breakfast at 10:00 am. Michael had arrived their first and reserved a table in the back corner. Jackie arrives 10 minutes later. She had on a casual red summer dress, cut low in the front. As she walked to the table where Michael was sitting, he had a big smile on his face. He didn't know what to expect, but he was just glad she didn't stand him up.

Jackie smiled at Michael and said hello. He responded, "hello to you too, you look beautiful Jackie". She said "thank you," just as the waitress came to their table and took their orders. While waiting for their food to arrive, Michael told Jackie to speak first. She cleared the frog in her throat and begin talking. "Michael I love you, however, you'll never know the pain you caused me. As a woman, you robbed me of my innocence about love through abusive behavior.

The verbal and physical abuse I endured from you that night, no woman should ever have to experience. Then the humiliation I went through when the police arrived. One of the officers who responded to call, had once asked me out a date during a traffic stop. I wouldn't give the officer the time of day, because I thought I was in a relationship with someone who loved me. I had to tell the officers it was my boyfriend who hurt me. Then when my friends and my sister saw me sporting your insecurity around my eye the shame was unbearable. Love is never supposed to hurt." She broke down crying.

As she spoke those last words, tears ran down Michael's face. He was remorseful, and. every word she had said, felt like a knife going through his heart. This pain he was feeling was something he had caused on himself. He took her hand and said baby "I'm so sorry. I don't even know if I have the right to ask you to forgive me, but if you could it will mean the world to me. I don't expect you to forgive me now, I know the wound is too fresh. In time, I hope you can forgive me. Even if there is no chance for us getting back together, I will settle for your friendship. You are the kind of lady any man would love to have as a friend. Your positive attitude always kept me going. He wiped her tears away from across the He moved next to her.

The waitress came over to their table and asked was everything okay. They both Jackie said yes. The waitress walked away from their table. Jackie told Michael being friends, for now, will work for her. They shook hands and laughed. The waitress brought their food to the table and they ate and small talk.

Michael told her about what had happened when he went back home to visit his family. He realized that most black men don't get counseling because of the stigma of being crazy is attached to it. However, my mom put her foot down and the entire family went to counseling. His dad was not thrilled about the idea however he went. During their session, his father had to deal with some issues from his past. His father was clueless about the psychological effect his dysfunctional behavior had on the entire family. Michael's father grew-up watching his father abuse his mother and he walked into his father's abusive shoes. Michael's mother was not going to allow history to repeat itself. It was a burden lifted off her shoulders when they went to counseling. There he was trying on his father's same abusive shoes with her.

"I wish I had gotten help before I put my hands on you. Nevertheless, I'm work in progressive and now I understand where a lot of my controlling behavior came from," said Michael. Jackie

smiled and said "at least you're willing to admit you have a problem.

That is the first step to change." They finish eating and Michael asked

if he could call her from time to time. Jackie smiled and told him yes.

A month went by before they went on a date. Things were

different, Jackie picked the place they would go. Michael had no

problem going wherever Jackie wanted to go. Secretly inside, he was

thanking God for giving him another chance with the woman he loved.

He phoned the therapist that Jackie had referred him to go see.

The therapist's secretary, TisaAjelas made an appointment for him the

next day. The therapist, he was going to speak with was a man named

Steve. Steve was radical with his treatment. The next day Michael

arrived for his 9:00 clock appointment expecting to sit his office and

have the therapist ask some questions. Steve entered the room,

introduced himself to Michael and said they were going on a field trip.

Michael looked puzzled. "A field trip," Michael asked. Steve

responded "yes." I take all my first-time clients on a field trip.

He took Michael to the graveyard and asked him, "Do you

know how many victim's lifeless bodies reside in this graveyard from violence? Not just domestic violence, but gun violence. As well as a medical illness that was caused by stress? Stress is an invisible bullet that kills slowly. One of the key components that most likely played a role in the culprit causing their demise was the lack of love. Try to imagine the life of a child who grows-up without hearing the word I love you or getting a hug. Instead, that child gets beatings, cussed at like they're adults and called names like dumb and stupid. That child, "spirit of greatness" is broken at a young age by the hands and mouth of someone who was supposed to love them. Then that same child grows-up numb to love and does not learn how to settle conflict without violence. Then some else's child has to the ultimate price, with their life. Women who are afraid to get out of abusive relationship lose their identities and some of them have to take medication just to function.

He told Michael to close his eyes and think of the happiest moments in his life while growing up. A smile came upon Michael's face. He told him to open his eyes and asked him what did he remember. Michael told him, he remembered the quality time his mother spent with them when his father had left her. He told Michael to draw from those happy memories and move forward. He also, to Michael to remember one important word, whenever an unwanted situation arises, it is "choice." You have the choice to walk away from the situation and deal with it later, when you are in control of your thoughts and emotions. Or you can confront it when you're out of control and deal with the consequences that come with it. Michael shook Steve's hand and said thank you.

He had a new outlook on love. They left the graveyard. Michael was silent on the drive back to the office. He made another appointment to see Steve next month. On the drive home, Michael couldn't stop thinking about that experience in the graveyard. That experience left him wondering what more could he do with his life. Three months went by before Michael started a non-profit foundation called, L.B.B.K "Learned Bad Behavior Kills." One of Jackie's best friend named Akilah, who was a lawyer had helped Michael establish his non-profit foundation. This was his way of giving back to his community in hopes that he could prevent another individual from taking the same path he did. Jackie, Karen, Janice, Roxana, Denard, and Peter all worked with him at his foundation. Michael went to several high schools, churches, prisons and social events promoting the L.B.B.K message. He was dedicated to the cause. Through Michael's visits to the prison, he was able to recruit three individuals, Larry, Cornelius and Andre to join his foundation once they were released. They had a way of captivating the audience through their life stories with a little humor.

Michael talked to the audience about domestic violence, gun violence and the destructive impact it has on the entire family. He explained to the parents how love can be used as a key to bring positive change into their children's lives. He would ask the audience, how many of them would hurt someone they loved, no hands would go up? Then he would share his personal experience while growing-up and want he did to Jackie. It was so quiet, that you could hear a pin drop in the audience. He told them how he got professional help, thanks to his mother intervention. Getting professional help doesn't mean you are crazy, you are crazy if don't get help and you need it. Jackie sometimes accompanied Michael on his speaking engagements and she would share the story about Kwowada. They made a hell of a good team.

Michael's criminal case was nolle-pros after he completed the anger-management course. The suspension from his computer job was over and he was back at work fulfilling his passion. He also, went back to work as a part-time fireman.

He learned about wholeness, through his counseling sessions with his therapist, Steve. Wholeness comes through healing your broken spirit, loving yourself and forgiveness. To continue on the path of healing, Michael sent Charlotte a dozens of yellow roses and wrote her letter asking for forgiveness for the pain he caused her. He never heard from Charlotte, nevertheless, he was able to forgive himself and move forward. His relationship with Jackie as a friend was on another level because for the first time he knew what love was and he learned that happiness was an inside job.

Made in the USA
Columbia, SC
06 October 2022

68507155R00121